What If? #4 Halloween Edition

Halloween Edition

What If? #4 Halloween Edition

ISBN:9798227000286

Edited by the authors.

Book covers, illustrations, book formatting, and book interior design by www.authorerikamszabo.com

Published by Golden Box Books Publishing, New York, USA www.goldenboxbooks.com

Credits: for free to use stock photos and art by Pixabay artists, and photographers.

When Creative Minds Question the Boundaries

When a collective of talented authors merge their literary skills and unleash their imaginations, a series is born to delight readers who crave thought-provoking stories and aren't afraid to ask the question, "What if?"

With each turn of the page, readers are transported to fantastic worlds where anything is possible, and every twist and turn leaves them eagerly anticipating what will happen next. This collaboration of creative minds brings to life a captivating journey for those who dare to question the boundaries of reality and embrace the possibilities of the unknown.

Stories

Burdens of Immortality by Erika M Szabo

She didn't want to live for centuries. All she wanted was one happy life.

The Guest of Honor by E.V. Emmons

A tale of two families: One family's halcyon life is tragically disrupted, while another plans the perfect Halloween party. Evil is a point of view.

Bitten by R.A. "Doc" Correa

In the days of the Roman Empire, a French peasant and thief learns the true horror of what it means to be bitten.

The Doll That Had It All by Lorraine Carey

A woman finds a spell to restore her youth but awakens a dark force. She must pay the price for meddling with magic. What is she willing to sacrifice?

Demon Child by Erika M Szabo

Lucas couldn't shake off the feeling that something was wrong. His sister's once gentle and curious nature had been replaced with outbursts of rage and violence.

Area Code 666 by James Harper

Steve Hyatt's job, chauffeuring mentally challenged clients to voting booths to swing elections, gets complicated when he receives phone calls from somewhere that should not exist.

Haunting Memories by Erika M Szabo

Spraining his ankle on a stormy night when an oddly familiar stranger helps him home, John's mind is flooded with long-forgotten memories.

He Watches by David W. Thompson

An ancient creature and an ancient love meet newlyweds John and Evelyn Barrow. Can their love survive Halloween's heartbreak and a promised destiny?

The Last Resort by Shebat Legion

A grieving woman meets a mysterious stranger and learns a valuable lesson.

An Elder Race by Karen Over

In the mists and moonlight of Halloween, be careful who you mess with. That kid you called a liar just might be telling the truth.

Organs for Sale by Erika M Szabo

After discovering that the Witch's One Stop Shop is selling organs, a group of kids are struck with fear. In response, Jack decides to become a vegetarian.

Fallen Angel by Martha Perez

Isabella is a fallen angel, paying for her mistakes in hell under the watchful eye of Satan enduring constant torment from creatures and critters. Will she survive?

The Pumpkin's Curse by Martha Perez

A spine-chilling, suspenseful thriller. Scarlett and Mom have nowhere to hide from the pumpkin's curse; they're desperate to stay alive.

Master Brahm's Studio by Shebat Legion

A master seeks to teach his students valuable lessons, but in the end, who will be the master?

Broomsticks and Chocolate

Trick-or-treating, a Halloween tradition, works because its unspoken rules are rigorously observed. If those rules are violated, who's better to defend Halloween traditions than real witches?

Late Delivery by Erika M Szabo

It's All Hollow's Eve, but an inconsiderate last-minute pizza order must be delivered, and Memy Yagen's legend becomes a chilling reality.

Headless by Karen Over

When it's Halloween along Foxfire Creek, you'd best not roll your eyes about the local haunt. Especially when you're messing with one of Miz Flora's girls.

Fall Market by Victoria Adams

Elenore lives a life in the shadows, hiding from a haunting past. Then one sunny fall day she is seen.

ERIKA M SZABO
BURDENS of
IMMORTALITY

After enduring three exhausting weeks of arduous travel through the rugged countryside, they finally made their way back to the magnificent palace. Aya eagerly anticipated the comfort of her luxurious quarters and the flock of servants who would cater to her every need and whim. At just eighteen years old, she emitted delicate beauty that had stolen the pharaoh's heart when he took her as his third wife only a year ago. Her flawless skin glowed in the sun, framed by luscious dark locks and deep, alluring eyes.

***

Although she had initially resisted the arranged marriage, it was a great honor and elevation in status for her family. Yet deep down, her heart still belonged to Tanamet, her first and only love. He was a low-status merchant, and they both knew their forbidden relationship could never be more than stolen moments of happiness during her time living in her father's house while Tanamet delivered his delectable baked goods.

On her wedding day as Aya said her final goodbyes to Tanamet, her heart ached with the realization that she may never see him again. But he promised to find a way for them to be together, and she clung to that tiny shred of hope as she was whisked away to the wedding ceremony.

Despite the grandeur surrounding her, Aya couldn't stop dreaming about Tanamet. She complacently followed orders and endured the middle-aged pharaoh's clammy hands groping at her and his wet kisses on her body. The marriage bed was only visited once a month, much to her relief, and when she became pregnant, the pharaoh showered her with gifts. With the birth of her son, Aya's status rose even higher, inciting bitter jealousy and hate among the other wives who could only bear daughters. Fearing for her son's safety and his role as her ticket to higher status, Aya surrounded him with loyal servants from her father's court. The palace was filled with intrigue and tension, with sharp daggers hidden in the eyes of two wives who held higher status than Aya's own. And though the pharaoh

8

doted on his son with joy in his eyes, he showed no interest in his daughters, who seemed to fade into obscurity after their births.

***

Aya strolled through the palace, her steps gliding effortlessly as three handmaidens followed closely behind. The grandeur of the long corridors never ceased to amaze her, with its breathtaking wall paintings and magnificent statues of the Gods. Her heart swelled with a sense of longing and nostalgia as she walked, each footfall echoing off the marble floors.

As they reached the ornately carved door to her quarters, Aya's pace quickened, and her eyes sparkled with excitement. The servants bowed and opened the massive door for her, revealing a lavish room filled with luxurious furnishings.

With a joyful smile on her face, Aya rushed inside and scooped up the chubby baby boy from the nanny's arms. She held him close, examining every inch of his healthy body. "Is he well?" she asked the old woman who had nursed her as a child.

"He is thriving and content," the woman replied with a warm smile, bowing her head respectfully.

Aya showered the child with kisses before gently handing him back to the nanny's care. "My skin feels rough and dry," she noted, turning to her handmaidens. "I think a milk and honey bath would wash away the grime of the awful travel."

The young women nodded in agreement and quickly scurried away to prepare the relaxing bath. Aya motioned to her favorite maid to assist with undressing her. "Ugh," she sighed wearily. "I feel soiled."

"You will feel clean and refreshed after your bath," the maid promised, handing her a cup filled with cool lemonade.

***

9

The piercing screams and chaotic yells jolted Aya awake from her peaceful after-bath nap. She stumbled out of bed, her heart racing as she spotted Tanamet leaning against the wall with a dark, sinister look in his eyes.

"How did you..." she stammered, fear coursing through her body. "What did you do?" she screamed, horrified by the sight of her loyal servants lying lifeless on the carpet, their once vibrant clothes now drenched in blood. "Where's my son?" she demanded, panic rising in her voice.

With a firm grip on her arm, he dragged her toward the adjoining room where the old nanny stood trembling, cradling Aya's baby in her arms.

Tanamet threw Aya to the ground and shouted, "You belong to me!"

She cowered before him, lowering her head and whispering through quivering lips, "Why did you kill my servants? What happened to you?"

"I died," he laughed. "And now I'll live forever."

"You're not the Tanamet I fell in love with," Aya whimpered.

"No!" Tanamet laughed again. "I was weak. Now I'm strong, and I do as I wish."

"Kill me, but spare my son. He's just an innocent child." Aya begged with tears in her eyes.

He took a step back and observed her with a calculating gaze. "Your son will be Pharaoh! But that old man can't touch you anymore. You're coming with me." The air hung heavy with tension as Aya resigned herself to her fate, knowing she had no choice but to follow Tanamet's command.

"Where?" Aya whimpered and shrunk back, but her coal eyes flashed with murderous rage hidden by her thick eyelashes. *This is not the kind and lowly merchant I parted from a year ago. He's a murderer!*

"We'll be together forever!" Tanamet shouted, grabbing her waist; he pulled her close.

Aya's body tensed as she watched the transformation come over Tanamet. His once gentle features contorted into a menacing snarl, his eyes glowing a deep, fiery amber color. As he opened his mouth to reveal sharp fangs glinting in the light of the oil lamps, Aya's blood ran cold. She recoiled in horror as Tanamet bit into his own arm and forcefully dripped a few drops of his blood into her mouth. The metallic taste flooded her senses, making her retch and gag, but before she could react, Tanamet sank his razor-sharp teeth into her neck with a ferocity that sent shivers down her spine.

***

For what felt like an eternity, Aya had been subsisting on a strict diet of only fresh blood. The thick, coppery taste heralded the beginning of her eternal existence as she remembered the fateful evening when Tanamet sunk his teeth into her neck and fed her his potent blood. But the feeling of immortality coursed through her veins, a constant reminder of that transformative moment when her fate was forever sealed.

Tanamet, consumed by his newfound power as a creature of the night, becoming a powerful immortal, had changed him in ways Aya could never have imagined - transforming him into a cruel and heartless monster who saw Aya as nothing more than an object to be owned. But she was no longer the timid victim she used to be when she was controlled by her family and her despised husband. Embracing her strength and abilities, she couldn't tolerate Tanamet's mistreatment. And so, one fateful day, she took action as he slumbered in their darkened dwelling. She paralyzed him by piercing his heart with a wooden stick with such ferocity that the sharp stick went through his body, pinning him to the bed. Gathering bundles of hay, she set fire to her oppressor's body and watched with great satisfaction as he burned to ashes before her very eyes. It was a final act of retribution, freeing herself from his grasp and taking back control of her life.

Her heart ached with longing to see her son again, and she was determined to find a way. Using the secret passages that one of the servants had shown her while she was still human, she managed to sneak into the palace under the cover of night. The narrow and interconnected passages were like a giant cobweb, with hidden doors concealed behind statues and tapestries. It was as if the palace itself was conspiring to keep her mission a secret. With stealth and agility, she navigated through the maze-like corridors, able to enter any room undetected. The adrenaline raced through her veins as she inched closer to her ultimate goal - to see her beloved son. She watched the peacefully sleeping baby but quickly retreated when the hunger for warm blood overwhelmed her.

In the eerie depths of the palace, where shadows danced and whispered secrets, she encountered creatures of the night. They prowled the dimly lit passageways, their glowing eyes reflecting the moonlight. In the daylight hours, they disappeared into hidden rooms and crevices, waiting for the cover of darkness to roam once again. One fateful night, Aya came face to face with Bahia, her beloved handmaiden who had vanished without a trace not long after their arrival at the palace. The others had searched tirelessly for answers about her disappearance, but all that could be found were wild speculations and hushed gossip. Now Aya understood why - for she, too, had become privy to the dark secrets lurking within the walls of the palace.

Bahia's voice held a bitter edge as she spoke. "I've been turned against my will, just like you, my lady," she said. Her words were laced with resentment and regret. "But unlike so many others who succumbed to their primal urges to drain and kill their victims, I swore to never harm a human, no matter how tempting their life force may seem."

Aya leaned in, her curiosity piqued. "How do you do that?" she asked. "Sometimes I can stop, and the human lives, but most of the time, my hunger is so great, and they struggle so much that I can't stop until I drain them."

Bahia's eyes flickered with ancient wisdom as she whispered her answer. "An old immortal taught me that all of us have the ability to mesmerize humans," she revealed. "We hold the power over their minds and can use it wisely."

Aya's eyes widened in understanding as she processed Bahia's words. She could feel the weight of her own desire coursing through her veins, a savage hunger for fresh blood that she struggled to control. But Bahia's words offered a glimmer of hope - if only she could learn to leave behind only dazed, living humans, perhaps she could ease the guilt and shame that consumed her. "Show me how to stop," she urged desperation creeping into her voice. "What do I have to do?"

Bahia's gaze was unwavering as she replied, "You need to look deeply into their eyes - it will force them to become docile, making it easier for you to feed without harming them. And when you're finished, look into their eyes again and project your thoughts to make them forget what happened."

Aya couldn't help but feel a sense of unease at the idea of manipulating someone's memories, but she knew it was necessary if she wanted to continue feeding without causing harm. Taking a deep breath, she nodded and prepared herself for the challenge ahead. "I'll try," Aya exhaled.

Bahia tightly gripped Aya's hand as they slipped into a secret passageway leading to a courtier's room. The air was thick with the scent of opulence and decadence. Bahia leaned in close, her voice barely above a whisper, "I never feed on the servants. If they were to wake up feeling weak from blood loss, it could lead to severe punishment or even death. No, I only seek out the rich and lazy freeloaders of the palace who can afford to spend a day in bed recovering."

Aya chuckled, understanding now why the pharaoh's advisor, Tunk, often looked so pale and frequently called for the palace doctors.

Bahia's lips curled into a mischievous smile as she motioned for Aya to remain quiet. They tiptoed closer to the sleeping man, his snores echoing off the lavish furnishings of his chamber.

Gone were the days of ravaging their bodies for sustenance. Aya had honed a more refined and graceful approach. With each delicate sip from the largest artery, warm, pulsing blood coated her tongue with a rich, metallic flavor that sent shivers of pleasure through her body.

Despite the inevitable challenges and struggles that came with their immortal existence, they found solace in each other's company - two kindred spirits forever bound together in an unbreakable bond, united in their thirst for blood and eternal life. Together, they roamed the land, drinking in its beauty and indulging in the dark desires of their vampiric nature. And as they gazed upon the mortals around them with envy and pity, they roamed freely. They reveled in their immortality, forever cursed and blessed by their insatiable desire for human blood.

Every night, Aya would silently slip into her son's quarters, her footsteps echoing softly against the smooth stone floors. She watched with pride and awe as he grew into a wise and benevolent pharaoh, his youthful energy giving way to a calm and confident demeanor. His people adored him, their love for him radiating throughout the kingdom. Yet, as time marched on and her son succumbed to old age,

Aya's heart broke into pieces, the weight of her grief almost too much to bear. The once vibrant and energetic young man was now frail, his bright eyes tired and clouded with age. As she watched him slowly fade away, Aya couldn't help but mourn for the loss of her beloved son, the great ruler who had brought prosperity to Egypt during his reign.

Bahia bonded with a servant who had been turned before her, their shared experiences forging an unbreakable bond. However, unable to bear the role of a third wheel in their relationship, Aya made the difficult decision to leave her homeland behind. Wandering through foreign lands, she encountered creatures of the night at every turn, each one leaving an indelible mark on her memory. Though she formed fleeting connections with immortals, her restless soul could never find a place to call home. As centuries passed, the weight of time and solitude bore down on her shoulders, burdening her with an eternal sense of longing and isolation.

Time blurred together in her mind, no longer able to distinguish one year from the next or even one decade from the last. Memories of her human life faded into the distant past, leaving only snippets and fragments behind.

After enduring the turbulent waves and treacherous winds of the vast ocean, she arrived in America as a stowaway on a luxurious ship. The sea foam and salty air clung to her skin as she stepped onto the bustling streets of New Orleans, her heart racing with excitement and uncertainty. Under the cover of night, she explored the city's vibrant energy and diverse culture, her senses heightened by the pulsating rhythms of jazz music and tantalizing scents of Cajun cuisine.

It was during one of these nighttime journeys that she stumbled upon Elizabeth - a woman whose grace and radiance left Aya spellbound. As they locked eyes, a spark ignited within Aya, as if their meeting was not a mere coincidence but something fated by a higher power. As they got to know each other, Aya discovered that Elizabeth shared a similar fate - both were turned into vampires against their will, cursed to live an eternity in darkness and forever thirsting for blood. This bond between them, forged through pain and loss, brought solace and understanding unlike anything else either had experienced before.

***

The night before All Hallows Eve, they prowled the darkened streets in search of unsuspecting humans to feed on. Aya's steps were slow and deliberate; her sharp senses alert for any signs of potential prey. But then, her attention was captured by a glowing window of a nearby bakery. The sweet aroma of freshly baked pumpkin pies wafted towards her, triggering memories of her past. Memories of the human Tanamet, the kind soul who used to bring her family these delectable treats.

A bittersweet sigh escaped Aya's lips as she paused to gaze longingly at the display of warm, golden pies behind the glass. "Oh, how I loved those pies," she whispered wistfully.

Elizabeth couldn't help but notice Aya's longing and offered with a sly smile, "Do you want to taste it again?"

Aya's expression turned incredulous as she turned to face Elizabeth. "How could I?" she asked, her voice tinged with both disbelief and sadness. "Even the mere scent of human food has made me sick for centuries." Despite her words, however, the alluring smell still tempted her from within.

Elizabeth's eyes sparkled mischievously as she spoke. "Oh, there's a way," she said with a smile. "My dear aunt was a powerful witch, and she shared her magic with me before she passed away."

From her pocket, she pulled out a small leather pouch adorned with intricate symbols and emblems. With great care, Elizabeth opened the pouch and revealed its contents to Aya - small, green pellets that seemed to shimmer in the moonlight. "This is her special

16

compound," Elizabeth explained. "Once a year, on All Hollows Eve, the portal to the spirit world opens. And if you take one of these pellets before midnight, you can transform back into your human form for a full day until midnight strikes again."

Aya's heart fluttered with excitement and disbelief. Could this really be true? She reached out and shook her friend's shoulders in amazement. "Are you serious?" she asked.

"Deadly serious," Elizabeth replied with a grin. "Do you want to give it a try?"

Without hesitation, Aya eagerly nodded her head. "Of course I do! What do I need to do?"

Elizabeth's laughter rang through the night as she explained the process to Aya, her words laced with magical possibilities and endless wonder. And as Aya listened intently, she couldn't help but feel like anything was possible on this mystical night. They entered the bakery, bought two golden pumpkin pies, and returned to Elizabeth's rented apartment.

"With just hours left until midnight, we must prepare ourselves. As the moon rises and the clock strikes midnight, we will swallow the small pellet and recite the spell. And for a full twenty-four hours, we will shed our supernatural forms and become human once again."

***

With bated breath, Aya anxiously counted down the minutes until midnight. Her restless fingers drummed against the smooth countertop, her body vibrating with anticipation. The silvery moonlight illuminated her pale, ice-cold skin, making it seem to shimmer like a frozen lake. "Just five more minutes, and I can finally indulge in anything I desire," she whispered to herself, a mischievous glint in her eyes. Her gaze was glued to the clock, watching each second tick by like grains of sand slipping.

17

As the final moments before midnight ticked away, Aya's mouth watered in anticipation of sinking her teeth into something other than the usual crimson liquid she consumed. Her memory was filled with the rich, warm scent of baked goods and spices, teasing her taste buds. She let out a contented sigh as she eyed the pumpkin pie sitting on the kitchen counter, its golden-brown crust beckoning to her. For now, it looked unappetizing with its dull orange color and crumbly edges. But to Aya, about to turn human again, it was a tantalizing treat that she hadn't tasted for centuries - its creamy filling and flaky crust were a reminder of human pleasures she had long forsaken.

Elizabeth watched her friend with a smile and handed her a small, green pellet. "Swallow this, and let's say the spell together."

They held hands and recited the witch's spell:

When midnight chimes,

And the moon climbs,

And spirits roam the earth,

It will be a painful rebirth

When your immortal body turns.

Indulge and enjoy, but only for a day,

When midnight comes, hide away.

When your body turns in pain,

You will be immortal again.

As the clock struck twelve, Aya and Elizabeth's bodies contorted in agonizing pain. Every inch of their skin felt like it was being seared by flames while a bitter coldness crept through their bones. They collapsed to the floor, writhing and gasping for air. The torture seemed never-ending as the seconds ticked by. They could hear their own screams echoing off the walls, blending with the relentless chime of the clock. It was a hellish symphony that seemed to have no end.

As the final chime of the clock echoed through the room, the excruciating pain that had consumed them melted away. With a deep sigh of relief, they were human again and could revel in their desires without restraint. The oppressive weight of their previous forms lifted, freeing their hearts to pursue whatever they desired most. The possibilities were endless, and they could feel the rush of excitement and anticipation coursing through their veins. It was as if they had been reborn, ready to embrace all of life's pleasures with gusto and abandon.

Aya rejoiced as she placed her hand over her chest and felt the comforting thump of her heart once again. In a moment of pure bliss, she closed her eyes and inhaled deeply, taking in the rich aroma of the freshly baked pie.

The first bite was a symphony of sensations. The delicate crust crumbled under her teeth, releasing the warm, fragrant aroma of cinnamon. The sweetness on her tongue seemed to awaken every dormant taste bud, while the subtle heat of spices left a tingling warmth down her throat.

The sweet and spicy flavors filled her senses, causing her to savor every bite with delight. For those brief moments of indulgence, she forgot all about her immortal existence and simply reveled in the joy of being able to taste something other than blood. This simple dessert was a revelation to her starved senses.

Aya devoured the pie with an insatiable hunger, each bite a small moment of bliss. She closed her eyes and let herself be transported in her mind to a time when she could still savor food without fear or guilt. But those memories when she held her son in her arms felt distant now, clouded by centuries of darkness and solitude.

As Aya's lips curled in content, she felt a deep sense of gratitude towards Elizabeth. Without her, these fleeting moments of pure pleasure and satisfaction amidst an eternity of darkness and bloodlust would not be possible. "Thank you, Elizabeth," Aya murmured, her amber eyes meeting the young woman's gaze.

A genuine smile spread across Elizabeth's face, her cheeks taking on a healthy, rosy color. "You're welcome," she replied softly, happy to have brought some joy to Aya's otherwise dark existence.

Morning came, and they stepped out to the sunlit street with shaky legs. "What if…" Aya whispered, holding onto Elizabeth's arm.

"Don't worry!" Elizabeth laughed. "You are human! Don't you feel it? The sun wouldn't hurt you."

"Yes, but...It's been so long…"

"Just enjoy the day," Elizabeth encouraged her friend. "Midnight will come soon enough," she said, and her expression turned sour for a second. But then she grabbed Aya's hand and dragged her to see the colorful Halloween decorations. "Look! Nearly every house has a vampire display. If only they knew…" she winked at Aya playfully.

Aya's eyes widened as she took in the delectable display of caramel apples, waffles with strawberry whipped cream, and pumpkin pie at the bakery store. "Let's eat everything!" she exclaimed excitedly.

"Easy there," Elizabeth cautioned, placing a hand on Aye's shoulder. "Remember, you're only human for one day. You don't want to spend it feeling sick from overindulging."

Aya nodded in agreement, recalling the times when she had eaten too many sweets as a youth and paid the consequences. "How about waffles for breakfast with a cup of hot chocolate?" she suggested, gesturing toward the nearby coffee shop where a pair of handsome young men opened the door to enter. The aroma of freshly brewed coffee wafted through the air, tempting her taste buds even more.

The blond man's gaze fell on Aya, and his mouth lifted into a warm, genuine smile. His body seemed torn between entering the shop or staying rooted in place. Yet his gaze remained fixated on Aya, his piercing blue eyes filled with admiration and interest. The sunlight caught in his tousled hair, adding a golden glow to his already striking appearance. A gentle breeze ruffled his shirt, revealing glimpses of toned arms and a defined chest. Aya couldn't help but feel a flutter in her stomach as she met his intense gaze. There was something undeniably alluring about him, something that made her human heart beat just a little faster.

Elizabeth's eyes shifted between the man and Aya, her gaze lingering on the man with a sly smile. "He's quite a handsome devil, isn't he?" she asked.

Aya's attention was suddenly drawn back to Elizabeth, her cheeks flushing at the teasing tone. "What? Who?" she stammered, trying to regain her composure.

"He likes you," Elizabeth continued to laugh, her eyes following as the young man finally turned and walked into the shop.

A heavy sigh escaped Aya's chest as she watched him. "He's human," she stated, her voice laced with longing and disappointment.

"Can't you just put aside your vampire instincts for a few hours and enjoy being human?" Elizabeth exclaimed her voice tinged with frustration.

Aya's eyes filled with tears, reflecting her inner turmoil. "And then what? Should I tell him I'm a vampire and drain his blood tomorrow?"

Elizabeth gave her a doubtful look, trying to grasp the weight of Aya's dilemma. "Wait...you mean to tell me that in all those centuries, you've never had a relationship with a human..."

"Not even once!" Aya cried out, her voice strained with emotion. "It's easier if we don't even go inside. I can't bear this overwhelming desire. As a vampire, I never experienced these intense emotions or ever desired a relationship." Her words were laced with longing and pain as she grappled with her conflicting feelings.

"What about vampires?" Elizabeth asked curiously, turning to face her companion. "Have you ever found anyone to love?"

Aya's expression turned wistful as she shook her head. "No, and besides my brief friendship with Bahia all those centuries ago and now with you, I've rarely encountered male immortals. And not a single one has been able to capture my heart."

"Yes," Elizabeth sighed. "Males are solitary creatures and fiercely protect their territory. That's why I chose this secluded street, with only a few shops nearby. It's far enough away from any potential rivaling territories."

Aya furrowed her brow in thought, then asked, "Do they ever find a mate? Or are they doomed to live alone for eternity?"

"Rarely," Elizabeth replied, her voice tinged with a hint of sadness. "Men are different when they're turned into vampires. They don't tolerate closeness well and refuse to compromise. I know of only two couples who live together and manage to get along because the women are highly submissive."

Aya sighed wistfully, her eyes lingering on the door of the shop across the street. "I wish I could stay human," she said, her voice filled with longing. "I remember human feelings, and I feel them now. Oh, how I wish to kiss that man!"

"Then go ahead! Kiss him, hug him, enjoy the moment," Elizabeth insisted, a mischievous glint in her eye.

"What about tomorrow?" Aya hesitated, her mind racing with the consequences of her actions. "Bite his neck and drain his blood?"

"Who cares?" Elizabeth shouted, a wild grin spreading across her face as she grabbed Aya's hand and started dragging her toward the coffee shop. "Let's be happy today!"

The bustling streets were alive with the sounds of early morning. Cars honking, people chatting, and birds chirping as they made their way to the café. The aroma of freshly brewed coffee mixed with the sweet scent of pastries filled the air, enticing them even more.

The tinkling of the door chime resounded through the quaint shop, causing a chubby, middle-aged man to leap into action from his spot behind the counter. His face lit up with delight as he looked at the two women who had just entered.

On the other side of the cafe, the two young men they saw entering the shop lounged at a small table, leisurely sipping their coffee and nibbling on flaky croissants. One of them, a blond with bright blue eyes, looked up and flashed a charming smile at Aya. She couldn't help but feel her heart flutter at the sight.

The shop owner greeted them. "Good morning, lovely ladies," he beamed. His enthusiasm for serving them was palpable as he asked, "What can I brighten your morning with today?"

"You said you wanted waffles with strawberry whipped cream and hot chocolate, right?" Elizabeth asked with a knowing smile. Aya could only nod, her voice caught in her throat, feeling the blond man's intense stare.

With a confident grin, Elizabeth turned to the shopkeeper. "We'll have two orders of that, please."

The shopkeeper beamed at them and gestured toward a small table by the window, offering a perfect view of the bustling street outside. "Right this way, ladies," he said warmly.

As they settled into their seats, the blond man stood up, walked to their table, and said, his eyes never leaving Aya's face. "Please excuse my boldness, but I couldn't pass up the opportunity to meet you ladies. My name is Peter."

Aya's cheeks flushed with a deep, rosy hue as she turned toward Elizabeth, hoping to hide her sudden girlish shyness.

The shopkeeper emerged through the swinging door, holding a silver tray with two steaming cups. The rich, decadent aroma of hot chocolate wafted through the air, causing Aya's stomach to grumble in anticipation. He placed the mugs on the table and said, "The waffles will be ready in just a minute."

Peter pointed at the chair across from Aya and asked, "May I?" He nervously cleared his throat before speaking again. "By any chance, are you lovely young ladies new to our charming town?"

Aya summoned her courage and lifted her gaze to meet his. "Yes, we're just visiting," she answered with a hint of hesitation. Her voice carried the weight of her foreignness in this unfamiliar town. "I'm Aya, and my friend is Elizabeth." She offered a warm smile, hoping to ease the awkwardness.

"It's a pleasure to make your acquaintance," Peter greeted them with a brief bow of his head, his demeanor welcoming. "Where are you from?"

"I was born and raised in Egypt," Aya hesitantly said, not including when.

"I'm from good old England," Elizabeth added quickly, afraid that Aya might say something more revealing.

"Have you made any plans for today? The whole town will be brimming with excitement and celebration, lasting well into the night. Halloween holds great significance here." His eyes twinkled as he spoke, adding a touch of whimsy to the conversation.

The excitement in Peter's voice was contagious, and Aya's heart raced with anticipation as she exchanged a quick glance with Elizabeth. Their eyes met and conveyed the same message: they were ready for an adventure. Turning back to Peter, Aya smiled eagerly.

"No plans yet," she admitted, "but we would be grateful for any recommendations you have."

As Peter spoke, his smile seemed to widen even further, encompassing the excitement of the day ahead. His words flowed like a river of anticipation, detailing each event with enthusiasm and delight. "The street vendors will soon start to set up their stalls, offering tantalizing treats and trinkets. The streets will come alive with people in elaborate Halloween costumes, ready to feast on delicious food and drinks. The haunted house will beckon visitors with its chilling mysteries throughout the day. As the evening approaches, trick-or-treating will commence in the enchanting French Quarter, followed by lively dance parties that will carry on until the early hours of the morning."

Aya sat on the edge of her seat, captivated by Peter's charm. His infectious cheerfulness drew her in more and more with each passing moment. A playful smile tugged at the corners of her mouth as she listened. "Sounds quite exciting," she said, trying to contain her excitement.

Elizabeth's eyes sparkled with amusement as she observed the exchange between Peter and Aya. Her lips curved into a content smile, pleased to see their mutual attraction.

Peter's brows furrowed in deep thought. Finally, he seemed to come to a decision and asked boldly, "May I have the pleasure of accompanying you for the day?"

Aya's heart fluttered at his offer, caught off guard by his confident manner. She blushed, feeling flattered by his attention. Her questioning gaze quickly softened into a warm smile as he eagerly explained his plan for the day.

"Me and my friend there," he nodded toward the table in the far corner. "We have the whole day to spend with you if you both like the idea." Peter's warm smile and charming demeanor made it hard for

Aya to resist. She blushed shyly before replying, "That sounds wonderful." The mere thought of spending the entire day with him sent a flurry of butterflies dancing in her stomach.

Just then, Peter's friend walked to their table. Peter's eyes lit up as he motioned toward him. "Paul, please come meet these two lovely ladies."

The handsome auburn-haired man approached with a warm smile spreading across his face and took a seat across from Elizabeth. He introduced himself while his eyes never left Elizabeth's face. There was a hint of admiration in his gaze, and he lingered for a moment longer than necessary when shaking her hand. Seeing the instant attraction between the two, Peter extended an invitation for Paul to spend the day together.

"I'll be happy to!" Paul eagerly responded. "Unless...the ladies object."

Elizabeth's heart fluttered as she quickly spoke up, "No objections here! Please join us. We don't know anyone in this new town yet." As she spoke, she felt a tinge of excitement at the possibilities awaiting them.

Aya and Elizabeth finished their breakfast and promised to meet the men around noon. The sidewalk was bustling with people dressed already for the festivities as they left the coffee shop and walked down the street to the costume shop, which was filled with hundreds of scary masks and colorful outfits.

"What should we go as?" Aya asked.

"Um...vampires...maybe?" Elizabeth giggled.

"But..." Aya hesitated. "I guess...might as well. At midnight, we'll turn back to one, anyway," she sighed.

After gathering the black dresses, capes, and makeup, they went back to Elizabeth's apartment to change. When Aya applied makeup to make her healthy-looking skin look bluish-white and fitted the false fangs on her teeth, her mood turned bitter. She wiped the makeup off her face. *Perhaps I should just stay in here. What's the point of going out? I'll be the same monster again tomorrow.* Her reflection in the mirror only fueled her bitterness as she clenched her fists and shouted at herself, "You're wasting the precious few hours you have left as a human! Instead of sulking and hiding away, go out and embrace the day, make lasting memories, and perhaps even fall in love."

Elizabeth embraced her friend tightly, tears of joy filling her eyes. "Yes, let's go meet those handsome men and revel in this beautiful day," she exclaimed. "We'll face tomorrow's challenges when they come."

Aya's expression turned serious as she posed a question. "Do you think we should tell them about our secret before midnight, or should we use our powers to erase their memories after we turn?"

Elizabeth paused, considering the options carefully. "I can't say for sure," she replied honestly. "Let's just live in the moment and see where fate takes us. Then we can decide together."

Their words hung in the air like a delicate web, woven with uncertainty but also excitement for what was to come.

As they rounded the corner, Peter and Paul came into view, standing on the sidewalk with an air of excitement. Peter was dressed as a pharaoh, his head adorned with a regal crown featuring a cobra head. His robes were intricately wrapped around his body, with the crook and flail tucked into his waistband. Paul, on the other hand, sported a pirate costume complete with a shiny sword and a black eyepatch perched jauntily on his forehead. Aya's eyes widened in surprise at their costumes.

She could see the effort put into each detail - the glittering jewels on Peter's headdress, the weathered look of Paul's sword. A sense of playfulness and adventure radiated from their outfits.

"I hope you're not offended," Peter stammered as he noticed Aya's shock. "I thought...because you said you were born in Egypt...but I can change..."

Aya couldn't help but smile at his earnest offer. "No, of course I'm not offended!" Aya came to her senses and hurried with a reply. "It was actually sweet of you to choose this costume."

An energy of excitement and joy emanated from the people around them, infecting them as they joined the lively crowd. The streets of the French Quarter were pulsing with the spirit of Halloween. Ghosts, goblins, and witches, their elaborate costumes adorned with sparkling beads and vivid feathers. Haunted houses loomed over the revelers, their eerie sounds and flickering lights luring them in. The air was filled with the mouth-watering scent of Cajun spices, enticing bystanders to stop at street vendors selling festive treats and colorful trinkets. It was a scene straight out of a storybook, where magic and mischief coexisted in perfect harmony.

Music poured out from every corner, a lively mix of jazz and voodoo rhythms that seemed to stir up the restless souls of the city. Dancers swayed to the beat, their bodies moving in perfect synchrony with the music. In between sips of their spicy drinks and bites of jambalaya, they twirled and spun with shouting, laughing people around them.

As night fell, an eerie mist settled over the streets, enhancing the mysterious atmosphere. The Halloween feast began, tables overflowing with traditional dishes like blood-red crawfish étouffée and blackened catfish. Candles flickered on each table, casting a warm glow on the faces of friends and strangers alike as they shared stories of ghosts and ghouls.

Amidst all the festivities, there was a sense that something otherworldly was present in New Orleans on this special night. It was said that the spirits of those who had passed would return to join the celebrations. And as the moon rose high in the sky, it seemed that even the living could feel their presence in this magical place known for its rich history and haunted tales.

Elizabeth and Paul were swept away by the energetic dancing crowd, their bodies moving to the beat of the music. As they danced, they could feel their worries and tiredness melt away.

Meanwhile, Aya and Peter found a secluded spot on the edge of the party, a bench nestled under a canopy of trees. The soft glow of string lights illuminated their faces as they took a seat. Peter leaned in closer, his warm breath tickling Aya's skin as he gently took her hand in his and looked into her deep brown eyes.

"I'm so grateful for meeting you this morning. I've never met a woman who could capture my heart so effortlessly," Peter whispered, his voice filled with sincerity. "I am infatuated by you, Aya."

She felt her cheeks blushing as she smiled back at him. "I like you too, Peter," she admitted. In that moment, surrounded by the pulsating energy of the festival and the warmth of Peter's hand in hers, everything else faded away.

A broad, happy smile stretched across his face, revealing a set of perfectly aligned teeth. But as Aya gazed into his eyes, she saw a flicker of mischief dance within them. "What if I were a real pharaoh and we lived thousands of years ago? Would you still be interested in me?" he teased.

A shiver ran down Aya's spine as she remembered palace royalty's opulent but treacherous life. She forced a playful tone in her response. "Only if you promised I'd be your only queen and not just one of many wives," she chuckled, but then her voice trembled. "And what if I were a real vampire? Would you still care for me?"

His eyebrows shot up in surprise. "You mean like those bloodthirsty creatures from stories?"

Aya hesitated before clarifying, "Not quite like that...but something similar."

The air around them suddenly felt charged with an unspoken tension as they both pondered the possibility of one of them being something other than human.

"If you were still the same person, with your striking appearance and charming personality, I could see myself being attracted to you and possibly falling in love," Peter admitted shyly, and then his tone turned playful as he continued, "Though if you suddenly came at me with sharp fangs and a thirst for blood, that might be a deal breaker." Peter chuckled but then grew serious, his gaze fixed on hers. "I've never felt such a strong connection to anyone before. Being with you is like finding a missing piece of myself. I would do anything to keep you close."

His words were genuine and filled with emotion, sending shivers down Aya's spine. She gazed into his eyes and slowly lifted her head closing the distance between them, pressing her lips gently against his. Peter's arms wrapped securely around her, pulling her close as they exchanged a passionate kiss.

But their moment was interrupted by Elizabeth's cheerful voice breaking the magical moment. Aya reluctantly pulled away from Peter, feeling the magic of their kiss dissipate. "I hate to remind you, Aya," Elizabeth said urgently, "but it's almost midnight. We have to go."

Peter held onto Aya's hand, not wanting to let go just yet. "Can I see you tomorrow?" he asked, his eyes pleading.

Aya bowed her head, hiding the threatening tears. The weight of her heartache was almost too much to bear. She fought back sobs as she whispered, "I'll be busy tomorrow."

"Please! Don't leave me like this. Promise me we'll see each other again," he pleaded, his voice quivering with emotion.

With trembling lips, unable to bear the pain in his words, she softly whispered, "We'll see. I'll be here tomorrow night…if I can." But before she walked away, Aya took one more look at the man who could make her happy, a lump forming in her throat as she sighed and turned away.

"I'll be waiting for you right after sunset!" he called out, his hopeful words echoing through the noise of the celebrating crowd.

Paul held Elizabeth's hand as if he would never want to let her go. "I'll be here waiting for you!"

"I'll be here…maybe. I can't promise anything," she said, pulling her hand from his grasp.

Aya's heart ached as she walked away with Elizabeth, knowing that the future was uncertain. *Tomorrow, I'll be immortal again and my human emotions, the attraction and longing for his kiss I feel right now, will disappear. But after I was turned, I still loved my son with all my heart! That means I'm capable of feeling love.* She held onto the small glimmer of hope as they were swallowed by the dancing crowd.

***

As the clock struck midnight, a searing pain shot through their bodies. Their bones cracked and shifted, their muscles and insides contorted and stretched. They didn't need makeup to achieve their usual bluish-white skin tone. Aya turned her gaze toward Elizabeth, watching as her once striking blue eyes transformed into a deep amber hue, mirroring the change in her own eyes from dark brown to amber. She let out a deep sigh.

"Don't be sad," Elizabeth embraced her friend, offering comfort and support. "We both made beautiful memories, and we can be human again next Halloween."

Aya's heart felt heavy as she buried her face in Elizabeth's shoulder. "But…I want to see him. I want to be with him," she admitted, her voice laced with longing. After a moment of silence, she realized that her feelings for Peter hadn't disappeared. "I never felt love for anyone since I was turned. I loved my son, but I thought it was because a mother's love for her child is different. I thought my human emotions would fade away, but they haven't. I still yearn to hold Peter's hand and feel his gentle kiss on my lips. How is that possible?" Her confusion and inner turmoil were evident in every word she spoke.

Elizabeth sat silently; her brow furrowed as she mused over their predicament. "I don't know," she finally spoke, her voice tinged with uncertainty. "But I feel it too. I want to see Paul again."

Aya's eyes lit up with hope at Elizabeth's words. "Do you think we can?" she asked eagerly before the weight of reality set in. "But they're both human..."

"Let's think about it later," Elizabeth replied, her stomach growling loudly to break the tension. "I'm famished. The human food has worn off, and we need to feed." She stood up, stretching her stiff muscles. "Let's go find some A-positive breakfast and get a good day's rest. We can figure out what to do later."

The moon was high in the sky, casting a soft glow over the street as they ventured out into the night, the promise of sustenance and a day of sleep guiding their steps.

***

As the sun began its descent toward the horizon, Aya sat on her bed, feeling both nervous and determined. Elizabeth stirred beside her, slowly sitting up as she sensed the approaching sunset.

Aya wrung her fingers nervously in her lap. "You know what?" she said, breaking the silence. "I'm going to meet Peter. I'm going to tell him what I am no matter what happens..." She trailed off, her resolve wavering slightly.

Elizabeth nodded in agreement, her determination matching Aya's. "Yes, I feel the same. If they freak out, we can always wipe their memories."

With renewed courage, they dressed and headed out into the fading light. The last rays of sun disappeared over the horizon as they made their way through the now empty streets. The sounds of the previous night's celebrations were gone, leaving behind an eerie quietness that seemed to envelop the town.

Getting close to the dark, secluded spot, Elizabeth stopped. "We can get closer to them behind those bushes," she whispered. "I want to hear what they're talking about."

With a hand on Aya's arm, Elizabeth cautiously led them closer to the hidden alcove. The dense bushes provided cover as they crept closer, their footsteps muffled by the damp earth beneath their feet. From their vantage point, they could see Peter and Paul engaged in intense conversation. The low murmur of their voices carried through the air tinged with urgency and determination.

"I can't lie to her," Peter declared, his voice firm and resolute. "I love her too much to hide the truth from her."

Paul hesitated before confessing, "I can't keep it from Elizabeth either." His eyes flickered nervously as he spoke. "She's so beautiful and kind; I can only hope she can accept what I am."

As they sat in the shadows of the trees, a car passed by on the street, briefly casting light upon them. At that moment, their bluish-white skin shimmered in the moonlight, and their amber eyes seemed to glow with a mysterious energy.

Elizabeth couldn't contain her shock. With a nervous laugh, she stepped out from behind the bush, pulling Aya along with her. "So," she said with a mischievous grin, "you two have met my aunty, and she shared her magic with you!"

The two men stared at them in disbelief, sensing the women's vampiric vibe.

"You're…and we're…Peter stammered, and his face lit up in a bright smile.

"Yes, it seems we all are," Aya giggled. "That changes everything."

Relief flooded through Peter, and he let out a hearty laugh, pulling Aya into a warm embrace. "Phew…and here I was nervous about how to tell you!"

"Me too," Aya admitted.

The smile faded from Elizabeth's lips. "Now that we all know, let's make the best of what we are until next Halloween when we can eat waffles again with strawberry whipped cream. Until then…we are who we are." She shrugged casually, though her voice had a hint of sadness.

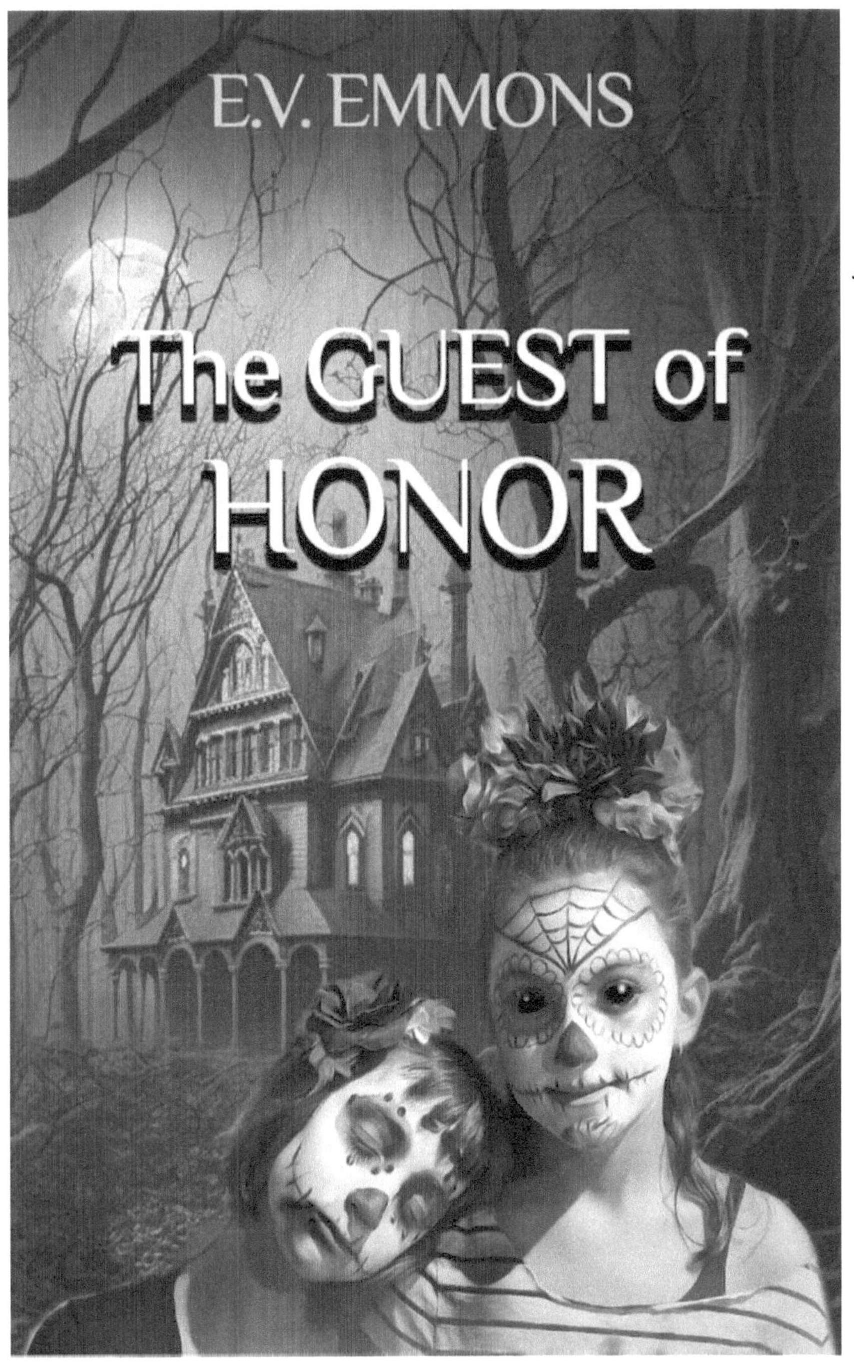

E.V. EMMONS
The GUEST of HONOR

Life on a farm is hard and if not for family, it would be lonely too. We cherished life in the fields, breathing in the rich, loamy smell of the tilled and mounded earth. We celebrated the sun and rain alike because we understood that both nourished the land, and what was good for the soil was good for us.

Months in the sun had turned our skin leathery, but we wore it proudly as a mark of devotion to the fields. At night, we were content to sit under the moon and soak up the warm ambiance from the porch lights.

Some nights, the sky would rain stars, and we'd sit and marvel at the celestial light show. The cricket songs lulled us into an easy rest until sunup when we'd do it all again.

One day, we noticed that the warm summer air had cooled, and turned the maple trees flanking the lane from green to shades of gold and red. In the orchard, the apples were ripe and round and shone like rubies. The animals feasted at their troughs, munching the dried corn. Abundance surrounded us, and we were thankful. All that remained was to relax and celebrate autumn and the coming winter, or so we thought. We had no way of knowing the horrors that lay ahead.

They came just before dark. One by one, with knives digging into our skin, they plucked us from our beds. Large, powerful hands crushed to our faces kept us silent. We squirmed and fought, hoping to get free of their vice-like arms.

Father, with his thick and burly body, wriggled loose.

"Get 'im, boys!" One man hollered. "Show that fool who's boss."

In seconds, they had Father pinned to the driveway, the pea gravel crushed into his cheek. Jeering and laughing, the three men took turns at his belly and sides with their steel-toed boots, and when that weren't enough to keep Father still, a crushing blow to the head stilled him forever. Pale, hard crumbs and guts oozed from the ruined flesh amid a rising fog of limestone dust.

"Load 'em up. Let's get outta here," one of them barked.

The thick burlap bags they shoved over us kept us paralyzed as they slung us into the back of the heavy-duty farm truck. They slammed the creaky gate shut and bolted it tight. Darkness smothered the truck bed, which smelled like rotten beets, manure, and cabbage.

Mother lay slumped atop a thin bed of straw, her body shaking under the burlap. After gathering the small ones close, we huddled beside her, hoping that somehow, we'd be of comfort to each other.

My insides quaked. With Father murdered and left behind to rot in the sun, what would become of us? He deserved so much more than to be brutalized and left for dead. He would never know a proper burial, a return to the earth he so loved. Visions of crows picking at his corpse and tugging at his entrails haunted me in the darkness.

The truck jounced and rumbled for a long time. It would stop, and then it would go again. We guessed they were taking us far away, and when the ride became smoother, we knew we had to be close to a town.

When they lowered the tailgate, sunlight flooded the truck. I winced through the burlap weave. They had stopped by an immaculately kept stone house. The patina of the stones spoke of centuries long past; this was a home built to house an enormous family—a home many would call a mansion. It was far grander than the house on our land.

The men dragged us from the back of the truck, directing us where they wanted with a rough grip on the dusty burlap caging our bodies.

"Filthy buggers. The boss won't like that."

"Not to worry, I'll take care of it."

After wrangling the little ones off the truck, they corralled us in a plywood enclosure with walls too high to escape. They ripped away our burlap sacks and blasted us all with icy-cold water until our skin ached and prickled. Being wet made the cold air so much colder.

"Did you have any trouble at the border?" The man with the hose asked our abductors.

The man jingling the keys to the truck chuckled. "Nah. Easy peasy, lemon, squeezy."

"Glad to hear they didn't give you any trouble."

The one who killed Father joined the pair and lit up a cigar. He puffed several blue rings into the cold, fresh air. "Well, shit, I wouldn't say that. One of 'em tried to be a wise guy, but we showed 'im. I don't reckon the others will give you a hard time after that."

The one who had been quiet until now drained the last of his *'BEAST ENERGY'* drink and whipped the crushed aluminum can at my head. "Made a right proper example out of 'im we did."

Unrepentant laughter erupted from our captors, and the sweet, weedy stench of the cigar hung in a loosely spun cloud overhead. We huddled together for warmth. Either the chatter grew further away, or we were too cold to listen when the screen door screeched on its hinges and slapped shut with a rude thud.

A plump woman with graying hair pulled into a tight bun emerged from the house, hastily wiping her hands on her frilly yellow gingham apron.

"Oh! Here comes the boss," the man with the cigar announced.

She wore a broad smile and had kind brown eyes, and for a moment, we dared to hope this woman was not a monster like the others. Once she learned what they'd done, she'd surely feel compelled to help us.

"You're back already! Show me what you brought."

We huddled around Mother in the corner. None of us dared to move. Our skin was freezing to the touch, but it had sunk far deeper than the surface. We shivered inside, uncertain if it was terror or the frigid air. Probably both.

The 'boss' peered in on us and ran her hands over the little ones. She even gave a couple of them a light, loving squeeze. "Very nice, boys. You've outdone yourselves."

The men shrugged and grinned, seemingly happy that she was happy.

"Well, you know what to do. Take the little ones into the kitchen. I'll get to them in a minute—those two," she said, pointing to Mother and me specifically, "introduce them to the kids—that ought to keep them busy while I get everything ready. As for the rest, you know what to do."

The two younger men disappeared into the house with the little ones. Mother and I clung to each other, even as the older man wrangled us back over to what appeared to be a shed but turned out to be a children's playhouse.

No sooner were we plunked down on the porch of the small playhouse than Mother fainted. She had always been a little on the fragile side. A ninja boy and two girls dressed in pink and purple fairy costumes emerged from inside, smears of peanut butter and jam still fresh on their lips and cheeks.

"So, kids, what do you think?"

"Whoah, cool!" The boy exclaimed. "Can we do whatever we want with'em?"

The girls eyed us curiously, and the youngest reached out to pet the top of my head.

"Yep, whatever you want."

"Can I borrow this, Papa?" The boy pointed at an ivory handle sticking out of the man's pocket.

"Mmm…sure, why not? Yer plenty old enough now. I was half your age when I got started. Careful though. Don't get caught runnin' around with it. You know what your Grammas like."

"Thanks, Papa, I'll be careful," the boy grinned and let out a sinister laugh as he struggled to drag Mother to the far end of the porch behind the wall.

"What about us, Papa?" The girls said, almost in unison. "What can we do?"

"You two, hmm…I know—how 'bout using the things Gramma gotcha in town last week from the big mart? You're always talkin' about doin' them fancy beauty makeovers. Here's your chance."

"Okay, Papa."

"And Katie, be sure to let Betsy have a go, too."

The older girl reluctantly agreed and ran into the playhouse, reappearing in seconds with a large pink-plastic multi-leveled suitcase on wheels.

The smaller girl, Betsy, seemed obsessed with petting my tough, leathery skin and poking at the scuff marks on my back.

It was surreal seeing this man who had murdered Father with the others only hours ago with his grandchildren. He was with them like Father had been with us. I wanted to cry, but the tears wouldn't come.

The man slapped the dust from his hands and waddled off toward the animal pens. The pigs snorted and squealed as he neared. I envied the pigs. I wanted to scream but couldn't find my voice.

Without knowing where I was or where the others were, I sat heavily on the smooth-planked porch, resigned to whatever the little girls planned to do to me. If I stayed quiet and cooperative, I might be able to form an escape plan. The girls were young and probably stupid.

What could they possibly do to me? I asked myself, almost smugly.

The older girl, Katie, took a black felt pen and drew several lines on my face. She then explained to Betsy that they would take turns coloring in the shapes she'd drawn and that she needed to do her best to stay inside the lines so that I looked good. They wanted to make me 'pretty.'

The two worked at 'making me over,' their tiny bow-shaped mouths puckered with determination as they colored. It was starting to get dark by the time they finished. They held up a mirror to me—and to my horror, long, white, jagged teeth protruded over vulgar red lips. Pink coin-sized circles marked my nose and chin. Black dots peppered my cheeks with what I guessed were meant to be freckles, and great blue eyelids with impossibly long lashes hung down from the bottom of my forehead. A pair of too-pointy eyebrows painted on with purple marker gave me a look of perpetual astonishment. I looked ridiculous.

"Something's missing," Katie said with a pout. "Oh, I know!"

She rummaged through the bottom drawer of the makeover kit and pulled out a curly neon-green wig. "Ta-DAH!" She sang out.

The pair arranged it atop my head, but not before cutting and ripping away my naturally curly strands.

Betsy clapped and hopped on the spot while Katie stood back to admire their work.

"She looks perfect now," Katie announced.

I had been watching and listening for any sign of Mother and the boy, but there was none. If she was still with him and where was anyone's guess.

"Supper's ready!" The old woman, known as the 'boss,' shouted and clanged a spoon against a metal triangle.

The girls shoved at me, urging me to move, but I refused and remained rooted to the porch. Once they understood that I wouldn't cooperate, they found the boy and a couple of his friends, and between them, they forced me into their wagon, and, with great effort, the lot of them dragged me up the bumpy path to the main house.

Parked cars filled the length of the driveway and the patchy grass surrounding the house. Orange twinkling lights stuffed into Mason jars like captive fireflies lit a path up to the front door. A projector beamed an array of ghosts, witches, and black cats across the exterior of the house. The music, a raucous piece about monsters, zombies, and mash, leaked out of the house like father's smashed guts.

When we reached the house, the cigar-smoking man carried me inside and plunked me down by Mother in the big room next to the kitchen by the window.

"Guests of honor are here!" He bellowed.

Katie and Betsy beamed proudly and explained to the gathering crowd that they had 'worked on' me all by themselves. Not to be outdone, the boy re-adjusted Mother on the shelf and announced, "My first carving ever! Cool, huh? Did it all by myself!"

The gathering of assorted witches, wizards, warlocks, and vampires moved closer to inspect the ghoulish handiwork.

I glanced over at Mother—sections of her skin had been flayed to create a patterning of darker and lighter flesh. She had been thoroughly gutted, and her insides scraped clean. Only the odd string of tissue dangled behind her eye sockets to suggest there had ever been anything more inside.

She had been lobotomized to give the boy access to light the candle he'd placed inside her body. The candle flickered with a possessing fire that altered her once smooth and blemish-free complexion into something demonic. The flame waned and waxed to brighten the fiendish new features the boy had carved into her face. If this weren't enough, he'd pressed a field of dress-making pins into the sections of her flesh that he had left otherwise untouched.

I wanted to scream, but the words and sounds wouldn't form—they remained a squeak in my head that only *I* could hear.

The crowd applauded and foisted countless accolades and compliments upon the trio of young children for their terror-inducing creations.

We were orphans now, our parents murdered by these terrible beings. It would fall upon me to look after the little ones. I had only been humiliated but was otherwise intact. I had to save them. There had to be a way.

The cows and pigs mewled and lowed under the barn's floodlight as the farm hands dumped the last of their buckets into the troughs. Through the large window, I could see the animals feasting on my brothers' dismembered bodies.

What was this hell? I wondered. My insides quivered.

Somehow, I had to gather the little ones and find a way out of this nightmarish place. But how? Where were they?

After the applause faded and the weird music set to a more tolerable volume, several remarked upon the delicious aroma emanating from the adjacent kitchen.

The air reeked of spices—cinnamon, nutmeg, ginger, and cloves—a terrible and nauseating quartet, and then I saw them, the little ones, my darling little ones, the last of my family…

Their tender flesh, which had been peeled from their bodies, filled a bowl near the kitchen sink. Several had been quartered and cooked and were still cooling in a pan—an ingredient to be added to something called 'chili,' while the rest had been baked into enough pies to fill the better part of the long granite countertop. Their pale, bony bits had been dried and salted and lived in a glass bowl beside the baskets of chips and pretzels.

The cigar-smoking man waddled past me and approached 'the boss.' "Say, Margaret, are you gonna make any of those pickles I like? Y'know, the stuff with all the cloves in 'em?"

"Of course, darling, but after Hallowe'en," Margaret said, indicating me and Mother's corpse across the room. "Don't you worry, I know they're your favorite. I wouldn't let the guests of honor go to waste."

Paralyzed—I couldn't breathe, speak, or cry. I couldn't wallow in my grief. All that I had, all that mattered, was gone.

I was alone now, waiting for this Hallowe'en while drowning in the putrid spicey stench of the pies.

BITTEN
R.A. "Doc" CORREA

O nce bitten, twice shy
August 28, 45 AD Provincia Romana

Francois slips quietly over the villa's wall, dropping softly to the ground. Crouching, he looks along the wall in both directions and then down the gentle slope from the wall to the edge of the woods. None of the Roman guards are visible. They all must be searching the estate's grounds.

Moving in the shadows, Francois cautiously makes his way down the hill. He avoids the bright spots of reddish light from the 'blood moon.' *We should have waited for the full moon to pass; there is too much light tonight.*

Wraith-like Francois disappears into the edge of the forest. He holds his stolen treasure inside his loose-fitting shirt. The cool, hard silver of the wine pitcher comforts him. *This could feed the family for a year. I hope Luc has taken something of equal value. That will get us through the next year.*

Silently, Francois follows the trail that leads to their rendezvous spot, a small knoll that is almost a league away from the villa. After half an hour, he gets the feeling he is being watched. The feeling stays with him, so when he is more than halfway there, Francois stops and listens.

At first, he hears nothing, not even a night bird. It is so quiet that all he can hear is his own breathing. The hairs on the back of his neck start to stand up. His heart begins to pound. Then he hears it.

The breathing is heavy and, at the same time, rapid. *Is that a dog? Has that Roman set the dogs on me?*

The longer he listens, the surer he becomes. *If it is a dog, it is huge.* Francois slowly turns his head, trying to find where the sound is coming from. He focuses on a copse of small oak trees to his right. Brush and tall grass grow around the trees. The sound is definitely coming from them. His vision zeroes in on the shadows between the trees, concentrating on a patch of bushes and tall grasses.

A flash of reddish yellow, then it is gone. *What was that?* Francois turns, facing the direction he is looking, and starts to crouch, keeping his eyes on the spot where he thought he saw the yellow flash. After a moment two yellow orbs appear, the moonlight adding a reddish tinge to them. With the appearance of the orbs comes a low, rumbling growl.

Slowly, the yellow orbs move closer, and the growling gets louder.

Francois draws his knife, taking up the fighter's stance his father taught him. He keeps his eyes on the approaching yellow orbs. As they draw closer the drooling snout of a wolf comes out of the shadows and into view. Its fangs are exposed, lips drawn back, and ears flat against the wolf's head. Drool drips from its mouth onto the ground.

Francois looks around, searching for more wolves. *Wolves always attack as a pack!* But there are none to be seen or heard. *Where are the others?*

As the wolf advances on him, Francois quickly considers his options. *I could run, but I cannot outrun him. If I fight, and I do not kill it quickly, the other wolves will get here and kill me. My only chance is to kill it quickly and find a tall tree to climb before the other wolves arrive.* Francois prepares to attack as the beast gets closer.

The wolf is about ten yards away now. Its coat might be gray with silver highlights, but it is hard to tell because of the reddish light from the 'blood moon.' It must be the biggest wolf to have ever lived. Francois guesses that it is at least a hundred and seventy pounds. As it prepares to pounce, Francois charges. For a moment, the wolf is surprised, but it recovers quickly and races toward Francois.

Francois rushes forward in a half-crouch, ready to strike. He realizes the wolf is going for his throat, so he leaps forward, going erect at the same time. The wolf's jaws do not slam closed on his throat. Instead, they clamp down on the silver pitcher inside Francois' shirt. He grabs the wolf's left ear with his left hand, twisting its head to the wolf's right, exposing the massive canine's throat. Francois drives his knife deep into its throat, all the way to the knife's hilt. The wolf howls in pain and leaps backward, away from Francois, wrenching the handle of the knife from his hand as he falls to his knees.

The wolf moves a few yards away from him and sits down, keeping his eyes on Francois. He looks at the wolf and watches 'smoke' rising from the wolf's mouth. *That cannot be smoke, it is cold, it must be steam.* Francois looks closer and it seems to him the wolf's tongue is burned.

While the wolf stares at him, it starts swatting at the knife hilt with its left hind paw. With a few swats, it gets a 'grip' on the hilt, pulling the knife free. The knife falls to the ground, and then the wolf swipes it into the bushes with its left front paw. What strikes Francois is it is barely bleeding. *Blood should be gushing out of that neck wound! What the hell am I going to do now?*

Francois starts crab-crawling away from the wolf towards some bushes when the wolf stands up and starts to walk towards him. His left hand lands on a fallen tree branch. He grips the branch, gets to his knees, and brandishes the branch like a club. Then the wolf rushes him. Francois waits until the wolf is upon him and swings the branch, smacking the wolf on the side of its head. The wolf's jaws snap shut on the branch, and Francois' left hand.

He screams as the wolf's fangs rip through his left hand. Francois grabs the wolf's ear with his right hand and yanks as hard as he can. The wolf just bites him harder.

Frantically, Francois looks for a weapon, any weapon to fight off his nemesis. In desperation, he reaches into his shirt and pulls out the silver wine pitcher. As hard as he can, Francois slams the pitcher onto the wolf's head. Again and again, he smashes the pitcher against it. After the fourth strike, the wolf yelps, releasing Francois' left hand. It tries to move away from him as Francois keeps whacking the wolf in the head.

Francois grips the pitcher with both hands and keeps hitting the wolf in the head as hard as he can. Though his left-hand hurts like hell, he keeps his grip on the pitcher. After several more strikes, the wolf falls to the ground. Francois keeps hammering the wolf's head until it stops making a sound, stops moving, and stops breathing.

He looks at the wolf lying on the ground. Clearly, the wolf's head is crushed, and blood runs out of its head onto the ground, pooling about the wolf's head and neck. The other thing Francois notices is it seems like smoke is rising from the wolf's shattered skull. *It cannot be smoke; it must be steam.*

Francois rips a strip of material from his shirt and wraps it around his injured hand. When he is finished, Francois scoops up the pitcher and runs off to the rendezvous spot before more wolves arrive.

Had Francois waited and listened, he would have known no other wolves were coming.

Had he waited a little longer, he would have seen the dead wolf revert to its human form.

Had Francois spent more time there, he would have known he was cursed.

Francois moves as swiftly as he can to the rendezvous spot. Along the way, he starts feeling sick. By the time he reaches the knoll, he has a fever. When Francois reaches the top of the knoll, he finds Luc waiting for him. "Francois, you're late." Luc looks him over and then asks, "Mon dieux, what has happened to you, mon ami?"

"I was attacked by a wolf," replies Francois.

"How did you escape them?"

"There was only one, and I killed it. I never saw or heard any others."

Luc responds, "You look like death warmed over mon ami. Can you make it back home?"

"Yes, of course I can, Luc; I just feel a bit ill, probably from fighting the wolf," answers Francois.

Luc clearly is not convinced, but they really do not have time to argue about it. Just like Francois, Luc knows that wolves hunt in packs. "We should go then," he tells Francois.

They move as quickly as they can back to their village, but Francois is feeling so ill the two of them end up stopping to rest often. They have to stop so many times that it is nearly sunup by the time they get home. When they enter the village, Francois is burning up with fever.

Francois sees his mother waiting near the gate as they pass through it. She walks up to them, concern clearly displayed on her face. "Mon fils, are you okay?" She touches his face. "Mon petit, you are burning up. What has happened to you?"

Francois tries to speak, but nothing coherent comes out of his mouth. Luc tells her, "He was attacked by a wolf, Madame Barteau. He killed it, but not before it bit him. He has lost a good deal of blood and has developed a serious fever on the trek home."

"Come, bring him to our home, Luc; once we get him there, go and fetch the rebouteux."

"Oui Madame Barteau."

Together, they help Francois walk to his family's hovel. Once inside Luc helps him to lay down on the pile of straw that is his bed. As soon as Francois is settled, Luc takes off to find the village's rebouteux. Francois' mother gathers rags and soaks them in cool water. Once they are wet, she lays them over his forehead. As she does, he mumbles, "Mama, I have it. We will eat today." Fumbling, Francois pulls the silver wine pitcher out of his shirt and tries to hand it to her.

She takes it from Francois' shaking hands and looks it over. Except for a few dents in the metal and the dried blood encrusting parts of the pitcher, it is beautiful. She takes a moment to admire the design engraved into the metal. "Oh, Francois, this is a wonderful piece."

"Mama, it…is silver. It will…feed the…family for a…year," feverishly replies Francois.

Madame Barteau asks fearfully, "Mon fils, is this your blood?"

Sounding more delirious, Francois answers, "No…mama, it…is the blood…of…the…wolf."

As Francois' mother worriedly gazes upon her feverish son, Luc returns with the village's rebouteux. "Louons les deux," Madame Barteau cries out at the sight of the rebouteux, "my son is maimed, he burns with fever!"

After a quick examination of her patient, the rebouteux instructs her, "Remove his clothes and wash down his whole body. Keep wiping him down." Then, she removes Francois' makeshift bandage as Luc helps his mother undress him.

The rebouteux examines Francois mangled hand. It has stopped bleeding, but yellowish fluid drips from the many puncture wounds caused by the wolf's teeth. It appears that some of the bones in his hand have been crushed by the wolf's powerful jaws. The skin of the top of his hand and his palm are torn, and the ragged edges are inflamed. "This is very bad; his hand could get a terrible infection." Francois winces as she pulls his hand close to her nose and sniffs the wounds. "I will try to save his hand, but we may have to cut it off to save him."

Though delirious, Francois hears her words; he gasps and sheds a few tears. He tries to pull his hand away from her but is too weak. "Mais non…I will…die a…whole man. You…will not…take my…hand!" Francois mumbles weakly.

His caretakers work furiously throughout the day as Francois goes in and out of consciousness. By evening, they are exhausted. Because they are so drained, Luc leaves to ask his mother and sister to prepare dinner for the rebouteux and Francois' family. They also prepare nutritious broth for his mother to feed Francois.

Stricken with delirium, Francois has the most vivid 'dreams' between periods of semi-consciousness.

Francois sprints along the deer trail, dodging bushes, and trees, racing the clouds, reveling in the freedom brought on by the light of the moon. He feels his heart pounding, his blood pumping, his bare feet thumping against the ground. His breathing is rapid; his exhaled breath becomes a mist in the chilly air. He howls as he comes upon the sleeping deer, scattering them in panicked flight. One thought fills his mind: Chase!

Francois focuses on a fleeing doe. He pours on the speed as he follows her down the trail to the creek. He gets close enough that he decides to take her down. Francois just misses her right thigh as his jaws snap shut on empty air. He comes to a stop to watch the terrified doe leap across the creek and scramble up the opposite bank, disappearing into the trees.

After a few moments, Francois walks over to the creek to drink. As he bends down, he takes in his reflection in the water. The face of a European gray wolf looks back.

For two days, he is in and out of consciousness, nearly mad with fever. On the third day, his fever breaks. The yellow fluid that had been dripping from his wounds becomes a trickle and, by the fourth day, stops completely. The morning of the fifth day Francois wakes with a clear mind and hungry, enough to eat a whole deer all on his own.

His family and friends are elated; they had been certain he was going to die, but now he is back! No one connects his recovery to the waning of the moon.

Francois' recovery amazes everyone and delights his family and friends. However, it does mystify the village rebouteux. She decides that she will keep a close eye on him.

By the seventh day after Francois was bitten, he has full use of his hand. The next day, all the puncture wounds on his left hand are fully healed, leaving barely noticeable scars. The rebouteux examines Francois' hand, manipulating it to check for functionality and to feel the broken and crushed bones within it. His hand works fine, and the bones feel as if they were never broken. The puncture wounds from the wolf's teeth healing so quickly have the rebouteux surprised, but she knows it is not unheard of.

After ten days, no one would have known that a wolf had attacked Francois, that the wolf had bitten him, that the wolf's bite had made him sick, or that he had been so close to death.

It is at this time that Luc comes to visit him. "Ah, Francois, you look well, much better than the last time I saw you."

"I am completely healed, Luc; in fact, I feel better now than I ever have before," replies Francois.

"Très bien mon ami. I have found another villa for us to rob," Luc tells him with a devilish grin.

"Excellent. When do we 'liberate' their riches?" he asks Luc, grinning back.

Luc replies, "We must scout it some more, but we will plunder it soon, very soon."

As they walk towards the gate, the village lookout shouts, "The Romans are coming!"

They rush to the open gate and look down the road. Francois declares, "If they recognize us, they will kill us and burn our village. We need to hide. Vixens avec moi, we must leave the village and hide in the woods without them seeing us leave." Luc nods in agreement, and the two men run to the other end of the village, slipping outside through the emergency doors. They move along the edge of the stockade to where it is nearest the woods and quickly slip into the forest.

All day, the two of them observe from a small hill beyond the tree line as the Romans search the village. Francois and Luc burn with rage as they watch the Romans torment their fellow villagers and trash everything as they search for the items Luc and Francois stole from the villa. They are not worried about the Romans finding them; the village blacksmith has already melted them down and cast the silver into one-ounce rounds. Then the blacksmith put the twenty-three 'coins' into a small leather pouch and gave it to Luc. Luc hid the pouch in the tree stump, near the stream the villagers use to water their crops, that the two thieves use to hide their loot.

It is evening when the Romans finally leave the village. By then, they had made quite a mess of the two men's homes. Francois starts to move, but Luc stops him. "We should wait a while, perhaps a day."

"Why?" asks Francois.

Luc replies, "Because the Romans are sneaky. I bet they left a lookout to watch for us entering the village." At first, Francois thinks Luc is being paranoid, but as he thinks about it, he decides Luc is probably right. So, the two thieves settle in for an overnight stay.

They watch from their hideout all the next day. Nothing happens until late afternoon that is when a Roman walks out of a patch of woods east of the gate. The man takes a long look at the village and then jogs down the road the way the Romans came from. Once he disappears, Luc and Francois start to work their way back to the village.

As they enter their village, they at once see that it is a mess. The Romans overturned all the carts, emptied all the food bins, tore down all the haystacks, and even dumped over all the wood piles. When Francois arrives at his family's hovel, he finds that the Romans tore it down.

He sees his father and younger brothers lashing the timbers of the hovel's roof together. *Mon père is too old to be doing this work.* Francois moves down into the dugout they live in. A quick look around shows him the Romans had destroyed what little furniture his family had. *Mon père made all of these!* Francois says, "Papa, go and rest; I'll take over this task." His father nods but does not go to rest; instead, he helps Francois' mother gather the thatch for the roof.

The villagers work for five days repairing the destruction the Romans had wreaked upon them. They must work from sunup to sundown, but they swiftly repair most of it. All of this has Francois furious; it also has him chastised. *All of this happened because Luc and I robbed that Roman villa!*

With all that has happened, no one remembers that it has been sixteen days since Francois was bitten by the wolf, except Francois. That night, he starts having vivid dreams again.

For the next eleven days, whenever they are not helping to get the village back to normal, Francois and Luc scout the Roman villa they plan to rob.

For the last six years, Luc and Francois have been 'successful' thieves because they do all they can to reduce the chance of getting caught. They spend days scouting their mark, finding every entrance, door, or window. They pace out the villa's walls to find where the easiest ways to get over or around them. Because the owners of these estates hire former legionaries or local thugs as guards, it has become essential for Luc and Francois to pinpoint all the guard posts.

They build a 'mock-up' of their target out of available materials in the woods so they can plan and practice the robbery. Francois and Luc take turns practicing the entry while the other takes on the role of guard. Though the thieves do not have a floor plan, most Roman villas have the same layout, so Luc and Francois have a good idea of where to go and what to look for when they get inside. This way every move has been rehearsed as best they can.

Though exhausted when he goes to bed at night, Francois has trouble sleeping. His dreams are so vivid that each morning, he feels like he did not sleep at all. The night before they select their rendezvous site and set up their final observation spot for burglarizing the Roman villa, Francois has his most vivid dream.

Francois looks up at the moon; it is almost full. He feels the breeze gently blowing over his body. He has never smelled air that is so fresh. The scent of the trees, of the flowers on the bushes, and the aroma of the grass all dance a delightful jig in his nose. The buzz of nighttime insects tickles his ears. All these scents and sounds, along with the moonlit scenery, create a rhapsodic euphoria within him.

He stands up and listens intently, seeking the sounds you can only hear in the night. His ears perk up; they capture the faintest noise. There it is. Francois sniffs the direction the sound came from; he drinks in the delicious smell. His stomach rumbles with hunger, and that starts him moving cautiously into the brush.

Silently, he slips from shadow to shadow, stopping every so often to listen to the night and quietly sniff the air. It has not moved; it is just a short distance away from him.

Francois crouches, gathering all his strength. His senses are locked onto the prey that is just beyond this last bush. He feels like a spring torqued down tight, ready to burst free. He takes in a deep breath and then releases all the tension built up in his muscles; with a single leap, he flies over the bush in front of him.

All one hundred and sixty pounds of Francois crashes into the warren, collapsing some of the tunnels. Terrified rabbits dart off in all directions. Francois spots a large one and leaps after it. The unfortunate pudgy hare is scrambling clumsily from the debris of its collapsed burrow, making it easy prey for Francois. His jaws clamp down on the hapless bunny, making a satisfying crunch as its bones splinter.

He gulps down his easily won prize, listening to the howls of other wolves seeking company in the night. With his strangely unsatisfying meal finished, Francois calls out to the others, but none of them reply. It strikes him that he is truly alone.

When Francois wakes, the faint taste of rabbit is fading away as his dream dissolves into the echoes of memory.

After he breaks his fast, Francois meets up with Luc, and they do a final check of their meager supplies and equipment. They have enough dried fruit for two meals each, two ropes and two makeshift grappling hooks, and a change of light-colored clothes to help disguise them if the Romans see them during the robbery. All this they put into their travel bags. They are both wearing the darkest colored clothes they own to help conceal them in the night. Luc tells Francois, "That's it, we're as ready as we are going to be. We should get going, we need to get there by afternoon so we can rest up for tonight's work." Francois nods in agreement.

They wave goodbye to their families, pick up their supplies and gear, and then the two thieves walk out of the village gate. After several yards, they move off the road and start to follow a well-worn deer trail in the direction of the targeted Roman villa.

The trail meanders through the woods as it rises towards the ridge line above the villa. It takes until mid-afternoon before they reach the rendezvous point. A quick examination shows that no people were there. Next, they trek to their final observation spot, a small hilltop about two hundred yards from the targeted villa.

As they get settled in, Luc says, "I'm going to grab a short nap; you've got first watch." Francois nods yes and then begins to watch the Romans. Luc quickly drops into a deep sleep.

For perhaps two hours Francois keeps watch, but it is so boring that he feels himself getting drowsy. He fights it, but his eyes keep closing. A couple of times, his own snoring wakes him. In the end, he can't fight it anymore. He leans against a mound of dirt and drifts off.

As the sun starts to set, Luc wakes. He looks over at Francois and frowns. *Francois has been sleeping so poorly the last couple of weeks I shouldn't be surprised. I'm going to let him sleep. I will get enough from the Romans for both our families. Sleep well, mon ami, I will swing back and get you when I am done.* With that thought, Luc turns toward the villa and cautiously moves down the hill.

It has not occurred to either of them that it has been twenty-nine days since Francois was bitten.

As Luc slips over the villa wall, the moon rises, shining its light on a sleeping Francois. This is the first moon rise of the three nights of the full moon.

He feels the moonlight teasing his face. His eyes snap open, and sees delightful splashes of light dancing among the shadows of night. Francois sniffs the air; the light breeze carries fragrances he had never noticed before. The pollen from night-blooming flowers, hints of mint, pine, and oak, and the heady smell of fertile soil. The distant flavors of rabbit, deer, birds, and bats season the stew of aromatic delights. Mixed in it all is a fleeting essence of roasting meat and the bouquet of man.

Francois rises and sits on his haunches. The light night breeze washes over his body, blowing his fur back and forth. He breathes in deeply, his heart pounds, and blood flows. All his senses are sharper than they have ever been. I have never felt so alive!

His stomach rumbles, angrily demanding to be fed. Francois' sharp eyes pierce the night, searching for prey. The scents of all the forest's fauna do not seem to him that they would satisfy the hunger within him. He remembers the unsatisfying feeling he had when he ate the rabbit in his dream. No, none of these creatures will fulfill his needs.

The direction of the breeze changes slightly, bringing with it the stronger smell of men. Francois turns his head in the direction the breeze is coming from. His vision locks onto a Roman villa. One thought fills his mind: FOOD! He gets up on all four feet and starts to trot along the deer trail that leads down the hill.

Luc waits in a bush across the road from the villa wall, listening for any sounds that he was discovered, but it appears only the night watch are awake, and they have not sounded the alarm. As he listens, he looks over the loot in his bag: two silver goblets, a silver plate, and two place settings of silver utensils. With satisfaction, he rewraps his ill-gotten wealth with the cloth he brought to keep the loot from making noise. Once he is satisfied, they won't bang together Luc heads back up the deer trail to Francois.

Francois revels in all that he's feeling; never in his life has he been so perfect. His hearing, his eyesight, and his sense of smell are all incredible. The strength in his body, the power of his stride, and the energy of his jump are all amazing.

As he moves along the deer trail, he hears movement in the distance. Francois' ears move to better focus on the sound ahead. He sniffs at the light breeze coming from that direction—a man. Francois starts looking for a place to hide.

As Luc moves further up the hill, he starts to feel like he is being watched. After another fifty yards, he is sure of it. Luc drops to one knee and starts to look around. The moonlight illuminates the surrounding terrain, but it also causes the trees and bushes to throw long shadows away from the trail. It is in one of those shadows that Luc is certain he hears heavy breathing. He tries to focus on where he thinks the sound is coming from. There is a sudden flash of yellow disks. *Were those eyes?*

Luc rises into a crouch and moves cautiously to his right as he draws his knife. The yellow disks reappear as a low, rumbling growl emanates from the shadow.

Francois stares at the man. His mouth waters, and his stomach rumbles with hunger. He can sense the man's fear, he can hear his heart pounding, his rapid breathing. Francois starts to move cautiously toward the man.

Luc can see the wolf's eyes coming closer, so he readies to receive the wolf's attack.

Francois charges, his feet pounding on the ground. He covers most of the ground between him and his meal in a flash. When he's just a couple of yards away from the man, Francois leaps into the air. In just a second, his forepaws slam into the man's stomach as his jaws clamp down on his chest. At the same time, the man drives his knife into Francois' chest.

The two of them crash to the ground. Francois rolls over the man's head, twisting as he does, snapping the knife from the man's grip. He rips a chunk of the man's flesh from his chest as he scrambles to his feet. He backs away from the man, chewing the chunk of man-meat as he does. In all his life Francois has never eaten anything that has tasted so good!

As he chews on the chunk of man-flesh, Francois sits on his haunches. While watching the man writhing in pain on the ground, he feels something uncomfortable in his left side. Francois brushes at his side with his left rear leg. His paw catches on something, so he pulls at it. He feels something pulling out of the side of his chest. With a strong stroke of his leg, he yanks something out of him that falls to the ground. He sees a hunting knife on the ground where it fell. As he swallows the chunk of man-flesh he's been chewing on, he uses his left forepaw to swat the knife into a bush, then turns his attention back to his victim.

He stands and walks menacingly towards his victim. The fear and pain in his eyes, the heady scent of his blood, and the promise of more man-flesh have Francois' senses swimming. His whole being is consumed by the power of making this kill, of snuffing out the man's life. In the back of his mind, Francois feels he should recognize the pitiful creature before him.

Francois leaps onto his victim's abdomen, causing him to cry out in pain as he does a partial crunch. His jaws clamp onto the man's sternum. He twists his head, yanking the sternum free and breaking the attached ribs in the process. The bones crunch in his mouth as his jaws crush them. He sucks the small amount of marrow out of the shattered bones, then spits them out. Francois greedily glares at the man's beating heart and starts to drool…

As a gentle breeze lightly brushes over his body and the first morning sunbeam tickles his cheek, Francois opens his eyes. As the terrible dream of the night before fades into nothingness, a sudden panic sets in; *It's morning! The villa, I slept through the night and didn't break into the villa!*

As he sits up, Francois realizes that he is naked. *Where are my clothes?* Looking around, he concludes that he does not know where he is. He sits on a 'bed' of decaying leaves under an overhanging pine branch. Clearly, he is not at the observation spot where he fell asleep. *Where am I? How did I get here? Where is Luc?*

An avalanche of dream-like images cascades through his mind. A terrified man fights a massive wolf. The wolf defeats the man, eating his heart. A flash of a face, the man is Luc. *No! Mon Ami!* A quick Look around shows Francois that Luc is not there.

Francois rises on shaky, tired legs. He is sure he did not sleep at all the last night. Though he is exhausted, he is not hungry. Francois starts to make his way up the ridge to the deer trail they were supposed to use.

It is some time before he notices that his hands are covered in blood. That causes him to stop and check the rest of him. Francois finds there is dried blood on his chest, his chin, cheeks, and around his lips. The shock of this discovery has him asking, "What have I done?" Francois continues to walk up the hill.

When he reaches the deer trail, Francois works his way back to their observation spot. As he enters the sheltered spot that they had chosen, Francois discovers that Luc is not there. Looking around, he finds that the clothes he wore yesterday are shredded, they lay on the ground in piles of torn rags. Though damaged his sandals are still usable, so Francois slips them on.

In his bag, he finds the spare shirt and pants he was going to change into after the robbery. He quickly puts them on.

Though this is not the rendezvous spot Francois waits for a couple of hours to see if Luc will join him here. By then, he is racked with concern, and he decides to look for Luc. Because it is daylight, and the deer trail is mostly visible to the Roman villa, Francois moves along the ridge just below the trail. This takes longer to traverse, but it is safer if the Romans are looking for them.

It is early afternoon when Francois comes upon Luc's mutilated body. As he looks upon the remains of his best friend, the friend he has known since they were small children, all those dream fragments come pouring out. Seeing the terrified expression frozen on Luc's face drives home the truth: it was not a dream; he killed his friend; he is the wolf.

"It can't be true; it can't be true!" Francois mumbles, and then he sees Luc's chest. His breastbone has been ripped out; the ribs have splintered. Luc's heart and liver are missing. "I ate them, Mon Dieux! I ate them!" Francois falls to his knees and weeps.

He does not know how long he wept. He knows he wept over the loss of his oldest and dearest friend. And he knows he wept because he has become a monster, because he is cursed.

Now there are no more tears, now his muscles ache so bad he no longer shakes from his grief. All that remains are his feelings of great loss and his self-loathing. *I am a beast, a demon from hell.*

As the dark of night settles in, Francois can feel the approaching moon rise. *When it rises, I will change; I will become the beast.* He stands and walks to a nearby tree. Francois removes his clothes and hangs them on a tree limb. He hangs his sandals next to them.

Slowly, Francois plods up to the ridge that overlooks the Roman villa. He knows his fate is fixed, that the first ray of moonlight will seal his fate. He raises his arms, completely surrendering to what is about to come, then looks down at the villa below. As the cursed moon starts to make its appearance, Francois shouts to the Romans in the villa below, "I am Francois Pierre Barteau! I am cursed! I am loup garou! I am werewo…Aoohoow!"

And the howl of the wolf echoes through the woods this night.

Lorraine Carey
The Doll That
Had it All

The bright Arizona sunlight permeated through the plantation shutters, waking Gemma Lowry from a restless night, which was not unusual considering her marriage was going down the tubes fast. Russell, her husband, had already left for work, which was normal with having to take over the accounting agency he'd inherited from his late father years ago.

Throwing back the fine linen sheets, Gemma walked through her vast territorial-style home and headed to the kitchen to get a cup of coffee before her usual morning walk. October in Arizona still meant warm mornings. She sat at the kitchen table, glancing out over the open courtyard at an unused chiminea that graced the corner. *I don't know why we never use this thing. Maybe it's because Russell has been so busy working late these days. Hopefully, with the cooler weather coming, we can make it a point to spend evenings out here enjoying the beautiful view of the mountains.* Her thoughts quickly turned to Russell and his behavior over the past year. Their daughter, Hope, was off at college, and things had indeed been different, but he seemed to lack interest in their relationship, and sex had become less and less frequent, if not non-existent. Gemma wondered if he was having an affair with his attractive secretary, who was young, blonde, and thin. After all, he was an attractive, well-built man five years her junior. *It's no wonder, can I blame him? I mean, it's not hard to notice the few pounds I've put on, not to mention my absence from the salon for some time. Did he also find me boring? Maybe I need to get back into teaching or doing some substitute work. That'd most likely get me back into my routine of dressing up and looking more professional. I guess this is what early retirement does to some people.*

Taking an early retirement was something Russell had brought up a while back as the business was doing well, and he had suggested for Gemma to retire from the classroom and do some private tutoring. After teaching for twenty-five years at the local middle school, she'd jumped at the idea.

After her morning walk, she decided to call her longtime fellow teaching partner, Lorna, and meet for coffee later that morning. Lorna had retired a few years back. Gemma needed a friend to confide in regarding her home situation.

Following a cool shower, she headed into her closet to select a simple sundress. After trying on several, she became irritated as most were all too snug. Looking in the bedroom mirror, she shook her head. *No more walks; I've got to cut back on those sweets I'm so addicted to or start running.*

She ran her hands through her dull red hair and fastened her long locks into a ponytail. She remembered the days when her hair was a brighter red. The Arizona sun did have its effect on redheads. She suddenly remembered she had some other outfits hanging in Hope's closet. Now that her daughter had gone away to school up north, she'd transferred some of her things into Hope's closet.

Gemma had successfully found the perfect summer shift, but her eyes were soon diverted to the boxes that housed mementos that were stacked in the back of the closet. She knew they were mostly old toys that belonged to Hope when she was a child. Feeling a strong urge, she pulled the top one out, finding old yearbooks and some of Hope's favorite children's books. She opened the second box and lying on top was an old shoebox labeled *Margie,* written in fancy script-style writing.

She sat on the floor, eager to open the small, tattered box. There was layer upon layer of tissue paper on top. She tore away at the papers, scattering them about the floor to find Margie, the fashion doll perfectly wrapped in silk and tied with twine. *At least my daughter wanted to keep this doll well preserved,* she thought.

She gently picked up the doll that resembled so many of the famous fashion dolls at that time, but Margie was unique with her long platinum blonde hair and sparking green eyes. She looked as though she was ready for bed in her white silky gown. Gemma couldn't help but notice the doll's brilliant emerald eyes. *I don't think anyone has eyes this color except for a toy,* she reasoned. *I remember when Hope spent endless hours playing with her and changing her into the many outfits I'd bought.* All the memories resurfaced from a different time, a happier time. She examined Margie, closely admiring all of the doll's youthful features. "You are perfect, you know. You never age nor gain weight. You have it all and don't even know it. What I wouldn't give to be in your shoes."

Gemma shook off this silly feeling and placed Margie back in the box, wrapped snuggly in her silk cloth minus the twine, feeling she didn't need to be bound up again after being bound up for all these years. She closed the lid to the box and wished her a restful sleep.

Gemma was looking forward to seeing her longtime friend Lorna again. The Coyote Corner Coffee Shop was not overly crowded for 11 a.m. They scored a back table and ordered their usual lattes and cranberry scones. A month had gone by since they'd last met. Lorna looked stunning for fifty-seven with her new short pixie cut. They'd been teaching partners for fifteen years at Brighter Days Academy and had become great friends as well.

Talking about memories of past teaching days was usually the main conversation, but today's topic would take a slight twist as Gemma was about to confide in Lorna about her rocky relationship with Russell.

Lorna listened with rapt attention and didn't interrupt until Gemma was finished venting. She'd offered her some sage advice and hoped her friend would listen. Lorna had suggested picking up a few more students for tutoring, knowing Gemma only had a fifth grader at the time. Gemma had commented that she wasn't motivated to get out there and advertise lately. Lorna had also mentioned that the two of them join the local gym. Gemma nodded, agreeing that both of these suggestions sounded promising. She reached out and took her friend's hand, thanking her and reminding her of what a good friend she's been after all these years and proceeded to ask her a heartfelt question. "Tell me truthfully, do I look older than 52? I mean, I want you to be honest."

"You look about right for your age, my friend. What are you worried about? You're still gorgeous! I mean, you still manage to turn heads."

"Thank you, but it's one head in particular I need to turn," Gemma replied, turning to glance out the window.

"Yes, you have put on a few pounds, but hey- we all have. It's all due to this menopause stuff. Some of it is unavoidable."

Gemma nodded in agreement, and the two had set a date to meet at the local gym next week and sign a membership. It was on!

During the drive home, Gemma couldn't help but think about Margie. Visions of the doll kept popping up in her mind. Somehow, she could feel the loneliness of this doll. She reasoned it was a link to her past and Hope's as well.

She arrived home and had to get lunch then prepare a writing lesson plan for Lindsay, her student. It was convenient to drive just a few blocks from her home in Scottsdale. Tutoring was always done after school hours. Lorna's words played over in her head about picking up a few more students, so she decided to phone the school after lunch and have them spread the word.

As Gemma was halfway through with her planning time, the same thoughts of Margie resurfaced once again. She left her office and headed to Hope's closet to retrieve the box. She opened it up and lifted the doll out. "You don't deserve to be hidden." Gemma decided to take her into the bedroom and set her up on the front dresser. She figured the doll would be an inspiration to her to take better care of herself.

The tutoring session with Lindsay was always a pleasure. She was a sweet girl but simply needed some direction. Lindsay had an assignment from school to write a page about being an inanimate object. It was fun and they both enjoyed working on this together.

Russell would be home in a few hours and Gemma hadn't started dinner yet. She did manage to marinate some chicken this morning and thought about making some fajitas and rice. It was a quick meal and would give her time to shower and get ready. She entered the bedroom and noticed Margie sitting on top of the white-washed Southwestern-style dresser. She sat against the tall leather jewelry box where Gemma had placed her. *Not a hair out of place, that doll*, she thought.

It had been a while since Gemma had worn something sexy for Russell, but suddenly, she had an urge to rummage through her lingerie drawer and select something. *Maybe this may spark up a romantic evening.* She opted for a white silky camisole and matching panties. *This will surely put a spin on dinner*, she thought then headed for the shower.

Dinner was ready, and so was Gemma, wearing her alluring outfit, and Russell was an hour late. Her cell rang and he explained his meeting with a client ran later than he expected, and he wouldn't be home for another hour. She sighed and told him she'd leave his dinner in the fridge for him.

Feeling distraught and stood up, she ate alone and then headed to the bedroom to change. As she undressed, she stared at Margie. "I guess if I looked like you, my husband would have been home on time or possibly even earlier. You don't know how good you have it."

What the hell was I doing? I mean, talking to a doll! I'm really losing it. No longer feeling sexy, she changed into her comfy nightshirt and headed to bed with a good book.

Hearing the door open, she knew Russell was home. She glanced over at the clock, and it read 8:30. She shut off the lamp on the bedside table and pretended to be asleep with no desire to interrogate him at this point. She was too tired to engage in a possible argument.

Russell walked over to her side of the bed and kissed her lightly on the cheek. Gemma kept still with her eyes tightly closed. He reeked of a jasmine-scented perfume, and she had no doubt it was Julia's. *That blonde temptress had most likely seduced him again. This had only confirmed what I had suspected. I'll bring this up at breakfast tomorrow.*

As soon as she heard his footsteps walking away, she sat up in bed. He'd left the hall light on, which illuminated Margie, sitting there as if she knew Gemma's thoughts. She stared back at the doll. *Did she?* She shook her head and drifted off to sleep.

Gemma made sure she rose early- early enough to confront Russell about last night. He was still in the shower as she slipped on a shortie robe and headed downstairs to make some breakfast. She figured maybe he'd be more likely to chat with a full stomach.

He approached the kitchen table, hair still wet but combed back neatly and dressed in his usual tailored suit and tie. "Mmm…smells good, hon."

"Thought you'd like a good start to your day," she said, setting a plate of over-easy eggs and toast down and then taking a seat across from him.

"And by the way, just wanted to ask you if you'll be late again tonight?"

He gave her a half smile. "No. I have no scheduled meetings planned."

"Oh, you mean no meetings with nicely scented clients?" she asked smugly.

He set his cup down. "Look, Gemma, if you're accusing me of cheating, let me set your fears to rest."

She met his gaze, ready to hear a lame excuse. "I met with a new client, and his wife accompanied him. She was heavily dosed with some exotic perfume. It even gave me a headache."

Hmm...I bet it was exotic. Gemma sighed and offered a quick rebuttal. "Well, lately, you have been working a lot of overtime. You used to come home by six, and we'd have dinner together. I can't tell you when we last did that."

He took a sip of his coffee and squared his shoulders. "Listen, I do realize work has been crazy lately, and yes, we haven't spent much time together. How about I take you out to dinner tonight? Go ahead and make reservations at your favorite restaurant. Being Friday night, it may be crowded. And by the way, I noticed that doll on your dresser. I remember how much Hope loved that doll as a kid."

"Yes, she did. I was cleaning out her closet the other day and found her. I thought she looked lonely in that old box and decided to set her free."

"Well, that was sweet of you. But you know she kind of gave me the creeps, like she was watching me get dressed."

"Oh, must be your imagination, Russell. She's just a doll."

Gemma walked over to the large French doors that led out to the courtyard, gazing at the glistening pool. *Did he really think a dinner would make up for all the lack of affection over the past year?* She took in a deep breath and agreed to his proposal. *Damn, he was good.* Those blue eyes always got to her, making her weak.

She had told him about her plans to join the gym and pick up a few more students. He agreed it was a good move to get her out of the house more but had to throw in a jab about the possibility of her losing some weight. She jabbed him right back. "Well, maybe when I get back to my desired weight, I'll get some of those hot-looking gym outfits and get some alluring looks from the other men."

"I hope you do," he chuckled.

What the hell is with him? She shook her head and turned her attention to cleaning off the table. He kissed her goodbye and reminded her to make those dinner reservations.

Feeling hopeful and excited, Gemma opened her laptop and made reservations at Granite and Ember Steakhouse for 7 p.m. It was one of her favorites. Not having to tutor Lindsay on Fridays gave her the entire day to herself. *Maybe it has to start somewhere*, she thought.

Upon returning from her walk, she headed upstairs to change. And there Miss Margie still sat looking as perfect as ever. Gemma made eye contact with her as she opened the top drawer to pull out a pair of new shorts. "So, Miss Margie, what do you think of Mr. Lowry taking me out tonight?" she asked as if expecting the plastic doll to respond.

Gemma had to admit she was looking forward to their date tonight. Once again, she rummaged through her closet, looking for something to wear. She managed to find a simple black sheath dress, the only dressy thing that fit her properly since she'd gained some weight.

It was still early, so she called Lorna and told her the good news. Lorna's voice was filled with excitement and reminded her that they were meeting next Monday to sign up at the gym after meeting at the coffee shop.

After checking her emails to see if there were any responses from the school for new students, which there were none, she perused YouTube when a few beauty channels came up with tips on how to look younger overnight. She laughed internally but brought herself to watch a few that promised immediate results by using various creams and potions. She read a few of the comments, and one in particular had caught her attention. It was from a woman who called herself Mystic Maya. She had posted her website in the comment section. Out of curiosity, she clicked on the link that took her to a site called 'Mystic Manifestations.' It touted the use of white magic and had various spells.

There were many members which seemed like some sort of a cult, men and women who had recommended some of the spells that were mentioned. Some of these ranged from attaining wealth, health, beauty, and the like. There was a moderate fee to access these mini-sessions, as this Maya lady called them. She read over the session for the beauty one, and it was more than interesting. This would be achieved in two sessions in the form of a video demonstration by Maya herself. Gemma sat there shaking her head and wondering why she was even reading this. *I mean, what if? Is this even possible? Am I that desperate?* These spells were similar to Voodoo and had her shuddering at the mere thought.

Surprisingly Russell had come home early to get dressed for their dinner date.

Both made some small talk on the way to the restaurant as Gemma inquired about Russell's day as he did hers. Gemma managed not to mention her researching spells and talking to a doll.

The table looked inviting, with a white tablecloth and a single rose in a crystal vase in the center. The lighting was low and added to the romantic vibe. Russell complimented his wife on her cocktail dress as they looked over the menus which had given Gemma a glimmer of hope. *Hmm . . . maybe I'll get lucky tonight.*

The waiter came to take the beverage orders, but Russell was distracted by a stunning blonde who sauntered by wearing a low-cut dress. Gemma had to pull him back in. "So, my dear husband, will it be white wine?"

He gave her that look, one that spoke of her immediate disapproval, but Gemma decided she wasn't going to let this ruin her dinner.

The steaks were delicious, and the Italian Tiramisu was even better. The conversation had been limited due to Russell's wandering eyes. Gemma had thought this was going to be a special night, one that would possibly rekindle their marriage. She glanced at the table across from theirs as a young couple was holding hands. *Would things ever change?*

Both Gemma and Russell kept the conversation pretty simple on the drive home. Russell had talked about a new project at work and had inquired about Gemma's tutoring. "Any bites on new students?" he asked.

She turned to look out the window. "No, none at all. I guess I'll need to make some flyers and drop them by the school."

Russell got a call shortly after they had arrived home and walked outside into the courtyard. Gemma stood there watching him, her hands on her hips through the huge French doors. He seemed to walk further away, possibly hoping she wouldn't be watching. *It's got to be business or that flirty Julia*, she reasoned.

Gemma headed down the hallway and into the bedroom to get ready for bed. Russell came in shortly after. She questioned him on the recent call. "Business?"

"Uh ... yes, it was that new couple I was telling you about. Just had some questions," he said avoiding eye contact, continuing to get undressed. "And by the way, do you mind setting that doll somewhere else? It still gives me the creeps the way she sits there as if she's staring at me."

Not wanting to give in to him but wanting to avoid a fight, Gemma picked Margie up, took her into the office, and sat her next to her laptop. "There ya go, Margie. You may even like it better in here," she sighed and walked toward the door but turned around when she heard a distant voice say, "Goodnight." *No—it couldn't be.* She headed back to the bedroom to find Russell asleep, or at least he pretended to be.

Saturdays were always free days for Gemma. Russell had his usual golf game, and Gemma did some shopping at the local market. After he left, she headed into the office with a second cup of coffee, planning to revisit the 'Mystic Manifestations' site. She looked at Margie sitting there still, wondering if she had actually spoken last night. She pushed that thought quickly out of her head and, without hesitation, paid the fee for the two videos advertised. *What have I got to lose?*

The first video was a demonstration of the items needed to perform a white voodoo technique. Maya called this one 'White Magic' due to the fact it was used for good purposes only. Her mild Jamaican accent added to the mystery. She was stunning for a middle-aged woman with her hair bound up in a satin purple turban and wearing a colorful caftan. It was clear she was experienced. This particular session claimed it would make one youthful again. Gemma watched with apt attention while Maya pulled out a plain doll made of burlap, white candles, pins, tissue paper, scented oils, twine, markers, a photo frame of some woman she claimed she'd found in a magazine, and some scented oils. She also explained that an Incantation Spell would need to be chanted, and an intention set by the person who wanted to achieve the results. It was a short one, and Gemma felt confident that she could do this in private while Russell was away—which was most of the time these days.

After lunch, Gemma had planned on watching the second video which was said to be way more detailed and included how to perform all the steps for the spell.

She watched as Maya used the photo of the beautiful woman as the desired result to be transferred to the burlap doll. She first lit all the candles and set the intention, which was a short chant but specified that each person would need to make a few changes so it would be organic in nature. She then proceeded to use the marker to write on the doll the fictitious name of the intended person to receive the beauty makeover. She also wrote words such as fair, wrinkle-free skin, small waist, lustrous hair, and brilliant eyes. She rubbed Frankincense oil and Bergamot on her hands then touched the glass of the picture frame, then rubbed it on the body of the doll so it would transfer the hair, skin, and youthfulness toward the doll. The photo was then wrapped in tissue paper and tied with the twine. A long piece of twine was then tied to the doll. This was to make an energy connection. Gemma had gotten a bit weirded out when Maya said one needed to be fully naked because clothing would block the skin contact with the oils. She did mention that she would not be undressing for this video. A bunch of laughing emojis popped up on the screen.

Maya ended the session with the same chant to close the spell. Gemma sat there mesmerized at all of this, chill bumps covering her skin with the mere thought of actually engaging in this sort of magic.

She grabbed her keys and was ready to head to the market to retrieve the special tools for the ritual when she headed back to the office to check her desk for some of the things that she might already have. She did find the pins and markers and was ready to head out when she looked back at Margie sitting there all perfectly and it was as if a light had gone off in her head. *Why not use her as the transfer doll? I mean, she is a real doll and one I would want to resemble as far as her looks went. She was gorgeous! She'd be the perfect vessel to make this spell work.*

She picked up her solid plastic body, shaking her head. "Sorry, girl, but you are about to become part of a ritual. I hope you will forgive me."

Thoughts of meeting Lorna at the gym on Monday had Gemma rethinking things. *If all goes right with this spell, why do I need the gym? I'll simply call her and tell her I've had second thoughts, and my legs have been bothering me again. I still want to meet her for coffee, however. I hope she'll understand.*

Russell was home early and volunteered to grill some steaks. He seemed to be in an unusually good mood. He came into the kitchen dressed in his khaki shorts and tight-fitting golf shirt, pulling out two steaks he had marinated earlier. Gemma fixed a tossed salad and popped a few baked potatoes in the oven, suggesting they eat out in the courtyard. Russell had agreed.

Gemma's hopes of a romantic dinner seemed possible now, so she headed to the bedroom to change into a red cotton sundress. It was loose fitting and didn't show too much of her tummy. She smiled and twirled around as she looked in the full-length mirror. A few naughty thoughts ran through her mind as she was hoping to seduce her husband after dinner. But she couldn't help but wonder why he seemed so cheerful tonight—h*ad someone else beaten her to the punch?*

Gemma thought candles would add a nice touch and headed into the office, knowing she kept an extra pair in the desk. As she passed by Margie, she thought she heard that soft voice again— the one that sounded like an eerie disembodied one. It sounded as if she said, "Don't trust him." She stopped at the door and turned around to see the doll sitting perfectly still. *Nah, just my imagination again.*

The dinner was delicious, and they both sat chatting afterward, enjoying another glass of wine. The fire in the chiminea added to the ambiance of the evening. Gemma moved her chair closer to Russell's, intending to give him some attention when his cell rang.

He quickly stood up. "Sorry, gotta take this, hon." He headed into the house and, most likely, to the office where she'd be out of earshot.

Thoughts about eavesdropping invaded her mind, but she reasoned she wouldn't feel the need to do so very soon so she busied herself with cleaning up the table and went inside.

Russell emerged out of the office carrying his cell. "I'm glad you moved that doll out of the bedroom but jeez, she still gives me the creeps when I see her. Can't you put her back in the closet?"

Gemma simply rolled her eyes at him, hoping he would get the message.

It was late and she suggested that the bedroom was now creepy-free so they could take advantage of the situation.

Russell said he wanted to watch a documentary on television. Gemma got the message; it was a no-brainer. She headed off to bed. Her hopes of a romantic night were quickly squelched.

Gemma was excited to begin her spell work on Monday, but not until she was home from meeting Lorna. Lorna had arrived before her and was waving her hands wildly from a table in the far back.

The smell of freshly brewed coffee and pastries had Gemma's stomach rumbling. Lorna looked stunning in her red yoga pants and matching tank top. Gemma reached out to offer a hug. "Guess you've decided to go solo, my friend."

"I sure did. I'm hoping maybe you'll reconsider once you see the results I'll be getting, but hey, you know I'd never push you into something you're not ready for. And besides, you are beautiful just the way you are."

The ladies ordered their usual lattes and scones. Lorna set her cup down after a few sips and mentioned that Gemma's demeanor was different. "You seem more positive today; I'd say a bit peppier. Things better with Russell?"

"We're working on it," Gemma said leaving it at that. *Well, let's just say one of us was.*

Gemma had at least four hours to spare before having to tutor Lindsay. Walking through the oversized living room, she glanced up at the wood-beamed ceilings and all the expensive Southwestern pottery pieces that graced the tables she and Russell had purchased on their many trips to Sedona. Those were happier times when they first moved into their spacious home. She headed to the office and opened her laptop to watch the second spell video again. The spell wasn't supposed to work immediately but claimed one should see subtle changes over time. This made sense and also would help to explain all of this to Russell. She already had some good excuses already lined up: some morning runs, visits to the local spa, and maybe a new wrinkle cream. She was ready and looked over at Margie and wondered if she was ready as well.

Gemma's pulse raced with anticipation, and nervousness set in as she closed the blinds in the office and set out all of the necessary items on the desk. Stripping out of her clothes and being naked wasn't something she intended the neighbors to see. She imagined what they would think if they got a glimpse of her unusual antics. She lit the seven white candles and turned off the lights. Since she had decided to use Margie instead of the recommended burlap doll, she knew she needed to stray from the initial spell as well. She looked at the doll. *I could do this.* Suddenly, she was overcome with a bold sense of confidence. It was uncanny how she knew how to make substitutions so well. *Maybe I was some sort of witch in a past life?*

With trembling hands, she spread out the fragile tissue paper on the cold, bare floor. The dim candlelight flickered ominously as she laid Margie's lifeless form upon it, her pale skin almost translucent in the eerie glow. Slowly, she took the permanent marker, its tip dragging heavily, tracing the outline of her body with painstaking precision, the ink soaking into the paper like blood seeping onto the floor.

Once the outline was complete, she cut it out with deliberate care, each snip of the scissors echoing in the stillness, sharp and final. The scent of Frankincense and Bergamot oil filled the air, thick and pungent, as she applied a thin layer to the cutout, the oil glistening ominously under the dim light. She pressed the oiled paper firmly against Margie's body, feeling the coldness of her skin seep through the fragile barrier. Her breath caught as she pressed down harder, ensuring that every inch of the paper clung to the doll, absorbing her essence.

Gemma's heart pounded in her chest as she anointed her own body with the same oils, the sensation both soothing and unsettling. With a deep breath, she peeled the tissue paper away from Margie and rubbed it over her own skin, feeling an inexplicable connection as the oils transferred from the doll to Gemma, binding them in this dark ritual.

The twine felt rough and coarse in her hands as she wrapped it tightly around Margie's body, each loop tightening the bond between them. With a shudder, Gemma secured a piece around her wrist, the final link in this sinister chain. The twine bit into her skin, a reminder of the conduit now established between them.

The room seemed to grow colder, shadows creeping closer as Gemma closed her eyes. The air hummed with an otherworldly energy, the anticipation almost unbearable. She could feel the weight of the ritual pressing down on her as she prepared to recite the chant, her voice quivering on the edge of darkness.

> *"By the shadows and the night's cold air,*
>
> *I claim the beauty you once did wear.*
>
> *Let it flow from your flesh to mine,*
>
> *With a binding force, dark and divine.*
>
> *No longer shall you hold this grace,*
>
> *For I shall take it in your place."*

Gemma felt a sudden rush of warmth running through her veins. The sensation brought on a familiar memory, similar to the dye the technician had given her before an MRI years ago. She did her deep breathing as she was instructed, still with closed eyes, only opening them when she felt relaxed, and her heart rate had slowed.

With much anticipation, she opened her eyes to see Margie still lying on the floor, her body glistening from the oils. Gemma picked up the doll. Margie had blinked her eyes. Gemma didn't know if she was imagining this or if it was part of the spell. She examined the doll, noticing she looked the same, but her eyes took on a luminous glow, ones that locked eyes with Gemma's.

"And you thought you were so clever with your research. You couldn't be happy with the body you had. No, you wanted something unattainable. You humans are never satisfied with what you have." The words came out, but her mouth never moved.

Gemma, horrified, dropped the doll, letting her thud onto the floor, her heart pounding with terror as Margie's voice, cold and disembodied, filled the room. It echoed, chilling Gemma to the bone. "You had no idea, did you? Your daughter and her little friends used me in a spell long ago, a séance to bring me to life. But they failed. Oh, how they failed! Silly girls dabbling in things they couldn't understand. When they realized their mistake, they abandoned me and left me to rot in that wretched box. You should have known what your daughter was meddling with. Dark magic never ends well! "

Gemma shook her head, chills running up and down her spine. "No, no! This isn't true! I had no idea— I need to close this spell with the chant again!"

"Deal with this, bitch! Now it's your turn to live in a box. One little perk is that you'll never age, always look the same, but I will become human now and live your luxurious life with that good-looking husband of yours. I'm sure he'll be happy to have a beautiful wife."

Gemma felt nauseous, and a dizzy spell caused her to fall to the floor. She could feel someone wrapping her up in a silk cloth and then tying some sort of binding tightly around her waist. Soon, all went black.

Russell decided to leave work early today. Lately, he'd been thinking about how his behavior was affecting Gemma. He still loved her and knew he should be thankful he had such a loving wife and a beautiful daughter. *I'm going to make things better*, he thought as he drove home.

He called out for Gemma, but no answer came. He went into the kitchen to find no trace of her or dinner cooking. *Hmm... her car was in the garage, and it was too hot for her to be on a walk now.* He headed to the bedroom to see if she was there. He stopped dead in his tracks when he found a strange woman lying on his bed wearing a skimpy white outfit. "Who... who are you?" he shouted; his eyes as large as saucers when he noticed this woman looked familiar. "You... you look just like that doll!"

Russell walked over to the bed, yanking the woman by her arm. "Where's Gemma? What did you do with her?" His eyes bore daggers into hers.

The woman held his gaze. "Don't you worry. She's right where she belongs. But you have me. You can have it all now."

DEMON
CHILD
ERIKA M SZABO

The Cunninghams had been blessed with a new addition to their family: a little girl they named Rebecca. She was a small bundle of wonder with inquisitive eyes that seemed to hold the wisdom of an old soul.

As the Cunninghams gazed down at the sleeping baby, their hearts overflowed with love. They marveled at how perfect she was, with delicate features and soft, downy hair. Just looking at her brought a sense of peace and joy that they had never experienced before. As they watched her sleep, they knew that their love for her would only continue to grow with each passing day.

From the moment she was born, every member of the Cunningham clan was captivated by her, but none more so than her older brother, Lucas. Lucas was only six years old, but he took his role as a big brother seriously. He watched over little Rebecca with unwavering dedication, always eager to lend a hand or a comforting hug. In his young mind, there was nothing he wouldn't do to keep his little sister safe and happy.

As Rebecca grew, her bond with Lucas only strengthened. They shared a room, and every night before bed, Lucas would read Rebecca her favorite stories until she drifted off into a peaceful sleep.

It was evident that Rebecca and Lucas shared an unbreakable bond that transcended time and space. They were more than siblings – they were kindred spirits who were meant to be together.

Lucas, as big brother, was always eager to teach Rebecca new things and protect her from any harm. When she took her first steps, he was there to cheer her on and catch her when she fell. When she started preschool, he stayed with her every day until she felt comfortable enough to make friends of her own.

And through it all, Rebecca looked up to Lucas with admiration and adoration. To her, he was the bravest and most caring person in the world. She knew that no matter what happened, Lucas would always be there for her.

Their parents watched with pride as their children's bond continued to grow. They were grateful for the beautiful relationship between their children and tried their best to foster it in any way they could.

But as much as they loved each other, like most siblings, Rebecca and Lucas had their fair share of arguments and disagreements. However, no matter how upset they got with each other, they never stayed mad at each other for long. Because, at the end of the day, they knew that their love for each other was greater than any argument or difference of opinion. They may have been different in many ways – Rebecca outgoing and adventurous while Lucas quiet and reserved – but overall, there was a perfect balance between them.

As years went by, Rebecca grew into a strong-willed child with a passion for learning and exploring. And through it all, Lucas remained her constant companion and protector.

But something happened on the eve of Rebecca's tenth birthday. Lucas was suddenly awakened by a loud noise that shook him to his core. His heart raced as he tried to make sense of what was happening. He jumped out of bed and ran to his sister's room and panic set in when he realized that the window had blown open and the shutters were violently slamming against the walls.

He ran toward the window and struggled against the force of the wind to close it; his heart was pounding in his chest. As he managed to shut the window, he turned to see if Rebecca was okay. His eyes darted around the room frantically until they landed on Rebecca's bed. Relief washed over him as he saw her sleeping peacefully, her chest rising and falling with each breath.

Just as he was about to go back to his room, he saw Rebecca sit up with her eyes still closed. She started murmuring nonsensical words under her breath. Lucas couldn't understand what she was saying, but it sounded like a language he had never heard before.

He watched in astonishment as a faint glow appeared around Rebecca, casting an ethereal light across the room. The wind outside seemed to intensify as if responding to Rebecca's words.

Suddenly, without warning, every object in the room began to levitate – books, toys, even furniture. Lucas's eyes widened in shock as he watched everything floating around Rebecca's bed. Before he could even process what was happening, everything came crashing down with a loud thud as Rebecca slumped back onto her pillow.

Lucas stood frozen for a moment before rushing over to check on his sister. He shook her gently, but she didn't stir. Because her face and body seemed relaxed and her breathing even, Lucas retreated to the corner and sat in a chair, staring at Rebecca until sleep claimed him.

The next morning, Lucas woke up with a feeling of unease in his stomach. He turned to look at Rebecca, hoping that last night's events were just a dream. But as soon as his eyes landed on her, he knew something was wrong. Her once warm brown eyes were now a piercing blue, almost crystal-like in their clarity. It felt like a stranger was looking back at him, cold and unfamiliar.

Lucas recoiled in shock and fear, his heart racing as he scrambled out of the room. He ran toward his parents' room, frantically knocking on the door. "Dad, Mom! Wake up! Something's wrong with Rebecca!" he shouted, his voice shaky and panicked.

His parents groggily opened the door, and Lucas grabbed his father's hand, pulling him toward Rebecca's room. His mother followed closely behind, asking him what was wrong.

"Her eyes! Look at her eyes!" Lucas exclaimed, pointing at the young girl who sat on the bed motionless as if in some kind of trance.

When they couldn't get her attention, their expressions turned from confusion to shock and concern. His mother quickly scooped up Rebecca while his father called his doctor friend.

As they waited for the doctor to arrive, Lucas couldn't stop staring at Rebecca's blue eyes. They seemed to possess an otherworldly quality that sent shivers down his spine.

By the time the doctor arrived, Rebecca had let her mother change her clothes, but her demeanor was cold and distant, and her eye color didn't change back to normal. The doctor examined the young girl carefully before declaring that she was perfectly healthy. "Hm…It's natural for babies' eye colors to change as they get older, but I've never seen such a drastic change happen overnight, especially at age ten," he mumbled. "But I don't see anything wrong with her; she seems perfectly normal. But just in case, have the ophthalmologist look at her eyes."

Lucas didn't believe it for a second. *There's something terribly wrong with her – this is far from normal. I see my sister's body, but she's not my sister!* He reasoned and tried to tell his parents, but they brushed it off as just his imagination because he was too worried.

"She must've had a bad dream, and the doctor said she's fine," his mother said. "Don't worry!"

"What about her eyes?" Lucas asked.

"We'll have the eye doctor check it. I'm going to make an appointment right now," his mother hugged him. "Everything is going to be fine."

Despite their reassurances, Lucas couldn't shake off the gut-wrenching fear that coursed through him, convinced that something sinister had taken over his little sister's body, and he couldn't shake off the feeling that there was more going on than anyone realized. And he was determined to find out what it was.

Days turned into weeks, and Lucas continued to have the unsettling feeling that something was terribly wrong with his sister. Rebecca's once gentle and curious nature had been replaced with outbursts of rage and violence. She no longer wanted to be close to Lucas and their parents; instead, she would punch and claw everyone when touched, screaming at the top of her lungs. Her once hearty appetite dwindled until she refused to eat anything but meat.

Lucas tried to tell his parents that something was wrong, but they were too caught up in their own worries about Rebecca's behavior to listen. They took her to countless doctors who all declared her physically and mentally healthy, and they said it was just a phase she would grow out of. Though the eye doctor was puzzled by the sudden color change, he couldn't find anything wrong with Rebecca's eyes either.

But Lucas knew it went deeper than that. He witnessed firsthand how Rebecca's tantrums seemed to have a strange effect on those around her. His parents argued more frequently and seemed to be under a constant cloud of tension and anxiety. The once peaceful atmosphere of their home had been shattered by Rebecca's screams and violent outbursts. Her once-beloved storybooks and toys were now torn and scattered across the floor, a result of her wild explosions, and the school psychologist suggested homeschooling her because of her disruptive behavior.

Lucas couldn't understand what could have caused such a drastic change in his sister. He wondered if there was something dark and malevolent lurking behind her increasingly erratic manners.

One night, while his parents were sleeping, Lucas heard noises coming from Rebecca's room. Worried that she might be ill or hurt, he cautiously opened the door to check on her.

What he saw made his blood run cold.

Rebecca stood in the middle of the room, surrounded by an eerie blue glow. Her eyes were glowing with an otherworldly light as she let out a bone-chilling scream that sent shivers down Lucas' spine. He backed away slowly, afraid of what his sister had become and what she would do.

As the months dragged on, the venomous rage seemed to consume the young girl. She took pleasure in hurling sharp objects at her brother and relishing the satisfying shatter of his beloved toys. More disturbingly, she seemed to enjoy biting and scratching her brother whenever she could get a hold of him, leaving behind angry red marks and bruises.

By the time Rebecca reached age eleven, their parents were at their wits' end. The mere thought of having guests over sent them into a panic, knowing the potential danger that Rebecca's explosive outbursts posed.

The one solace Rebecca found was in drawing and painting, but it was a twisted form of therapy. She would create intricate drawings of floating demons only to violently scribble over them again and again until the paper tore apart beneath her frantic strokes. Yet every time, the subject of her art remained the same - two misty demonic figures trapped in an unending cycle of being drawn and erased, a haunting reflection of Rebecca's own inner turmoil.

One afternoon, Rebecca seemed calmer than usual, and Lucas mustered up the courage to finally ask her about the drawings. But as soon as he mentioned it, her calm facade shattered and gave way to a twisted, sinister expression. She grabbed his hand, her clutch stronger than a grown man's grip, and revealed with chilling conviction, "They're my real family. One day, I will join them and kill you all."

A wave of terror washed over Lucas as he tried to reason with her, reminding her that their parents were in the kitchen. But before he could finish, Rebecca's eyes rolled back into her head. She lunged at him with a sharpened pencil, stabbing his face and throat with frenzied force. Blood sprayed across her dress as Lucas's agonized screams echoed through the room, drowned out only by Rebecca's maniacal laughter.

Their parents burst into the room and were immediately met with a sight that shook them to their core. Their beloved son was lying on the carpet, blood pooling around his battered body, while their own flesh and blood daughter was standing over him, a menacing glint in her piercing blue eyes. Without hesitation, they scooped up their barely conscious boy and rushed him out of the room, locking the door behind them. They heard Rebecca throwing furniture and screaming at the top of her lungs. The ambulance came, and they took Lucas to the hospital. And then, the second ambulance came. They first sedated Rebecca and then rushed her to the mental ward.

As their parents anxiously waited, tears streaming down their faces, they couldn't help but wonder where they had gone wrong in raising a daughter who could inflict such a brutal attack upon her own brother. Their minds were consumed with guilt and sorrow.

***

In the following two years, Rebecca's violent behavior continued despite the strong medications, and she spent short periods in the hospital under close supervision. The psychiatrists were puzzled by her condition and tried numerous treatments with no result. When she seemed calmer, they discharged her, but she had twenty-four-hour supervision at home by nurses who specialized in caring for the mentally ill.

On the eve of Rebecca's thirteenth birthday, Lucas was yanked from a deep sleep by the sound of shutters violently slamming against the walls in Rebecca's bedroom across the hall. His heart lurched with terror as he sprang out of bed and sprinted to Rebecca's room, adrenaline pumping through his veins. With every step closer to her door, Lucas could feel his fear intensify, his mind racing with worst-case scenarios.

The moment he stepped into the room, his heart skipped a beat as he took in the shattered windows and scattered glass shards glistening everywhere like fallen stars. The nurse lay motionless on the floor. Panic seized Lucas as his eyes darted to his little sister, who sat upright on the bed, her body contorted in unnatural angles as she muttered incoherently, her once bright blue eyes now a warm brown color. A gut-wrenching fear seized Lucas as he reached for her, his hand trembling.

Their parents burst into the room, drawn by the commotion. Rebecca turned to them with an angelic smile on her face, something they hadn't seen in a long time. *This is my sister! I can feel it*. Lucas rejoiced. They all held each other tightly while the ambulance was called, and the paramedic examined the nurse who regained consciousness.

"She managed to sneak up on me…and hit the back of my head," the nurse recalled, wincing in pain as she touched her head.

"You have a concussion," the paramedic declared, and they took the nurse to the ER.

As days turned into weeks, doctors and psychologists were unable to provide any reasonable answer or explanation. "This is a mystery that would remain unsolved," they all said.

Although they were happy about the positive change, Rebecca's parents were afraid and always on edge, constantly watching their daughter's behavior for any change. Rebecca was sweet and loving toward her brother and couldn't understand why Lucas didn't fully trust her like when they were younger. The tight bond between them was broken. Lucas tried to explain, but Rebecca kept saying that she couldn't remember much, and the past three years were as if she was in a jumbled dream.

The spiritual advisor's words echoed through the devastated family's minds, chilling their blood. According to her, the blue-eyed terror that had plagued them for years was not their child – it was an evil demon occupying their daughter's body. They were lucky the real child proved to be stronger and emerged before it was too late - before the dark demon's malevolent nature completely consumed her.

***

Rebecca could recall only blurred memories of the years while the demon was in power. She could barely recall the feeling of dread as the malevolent demon entered her body. She remembered bits and pieces of the constant turmoil inside her mind as she fought to be free.

However, she clearly remembered the day when the demon finally left her body and floated out the window. Looking into the demon's cold and lifeless eyes sent shivers down her spine as the eerie figure floated above the bushes, its piercing blue eyes peering into her soul.

The demon's grin twisted into a malicious sneer and its eyes locked onto Rebecca's with a disturbing intensity as it taunted her in a voice that dripped with hatred. "You won this time; your mind is strong. But I'll be seeing you again soon, and your body and soul will be mine," it cackled.

The words burned into Rebecca's mind, a terrifying promise of a bleak future. "No!" she screamed. "I'm stronger than you will ever be, and you will never enter my body again."

"We'll see," the demon hissed before vanishing back into the dark realm of demons.

Area Code
666
JAMES HARPER

The two men moved with deliberation, their forks passing through the food — Chinese for one, Mexican for the other — as they brought the rice and seasoned meat to their mouths in measured, slow movements, hunched over the tiny mock stone table in the main corridor of Lakeforest Mall. The short one, whose features displayed a ruddy, overweight look, stared at the meal without interest.

His companion, a tall black man with the shoulders of a linebacker and a close-cropped buzz cut, dipped and drew at the same rate of speed as if the time to consume the contents of the Styrofoam platter knew no outward bounds.

Another man approached, a pair of paper cups in his hands, the straws jutting upward. As he placed them before the men, he said, "Here you go, guys." Then he stiffened.

His phone buzzing from his pocket, Steve Hyatt stopped to reach down and then switched it off to prevent the vibration from tickling his thigh. Only later, after he'd finished feeding the 'tards, did he look to see who called, blinking as he saw the number.

"What the fuck?"

The call read from Area Code 666. Steve stared at it, blinked again, then turned the phone upside down as if to fix the aberration. The number did not change.

He spoke aloud. "Somebody's fucking with me." The men, William and Demetri, did not respond, pursuing the earnest consumption of their lunch in continued single-minded silence. Hyatt had long past caring about his language in front of his charges, his supervisors indicating that, while it fell into the area of a technical violation of established protocol, his position as caregiver faced little effect or consequence as they would not comprehend the language.

Tempted to call the number back just to see whether it went to a live line, Hyatt dismissed the notion on its heels as he shrugged. Probably a gimmick. Goddamn corporations would do anything these days to get you to answer the phone.

"Hey, Steve."

He looked from his cell to his new co-worker, Rachel Brockmeyer. He pocketed his phone.

"Hey. Sup?"

"Hey, so what's the deal with the schedule tomorrow? How we gonna handle the day?"

"It's all gonna be different. We're gonna spend the whole day carting them around to the voting places. You and me, that's it."

"Just the two of us?"

"Just like that old song, fam. We gonna be taking the entire clientele –"

"Every client?"

Hyatt nodded. "Every one of them, every single one."

"How many is that?"

"Few hundred."

"Fuck."

"Fuck, indeed. We gotta pick 'em up at all the designated houses, then haul 'em to the voting booths."

"Then what?"

"Then we march 'em to the booths, hand 'em the written instructions, and cross our fingers."

"And you say no one's caught on?"

"Not so far," Hyatt leaned toward Brockmeyer's quizzical face, "Runs like clockwork."

"Okay, if you say so."

"Look, stop worrying. I have been doing this for like six years. Easy- peasy –"

"You're making me queasy. Gotchu."

That night, after they saw the clients to their rooms to sleep, Hyatt retired to his within the halfway house, a Spartan affair that he kept furnished to a minimum on purpose. Hyatt felt his phone vibrate in his pocket. He knew what it would read even before he withdrew it. He pulled it from his jeans anyway.

Area Code 666. The same number.

"Fuck."

He stared at it as it buzzed in his palm. How could anyone even get this authorized? Aren't there some kinds of laws against it? Wouldn't the religious community object?

He moved his thumb to press Answer when the call ended. He whispered a curse as he placed the cell on his nightstand.

Distracted, he surfed his TV, his mind darting from one possibility to another on who or how any phone call could come from Area Code 666. An elaborate practical joke? A sick promotion scheme? A poor business decision? None of the ideas he came up with provided a real answer.

He reached for his phone to Google a search. As his hand extended outward, the phone buzzed with a text.

Steve, we need to talk.

It came from the same number. He held the phone in disbelief, not knowing whether to text back or ignore it. He chose to ignore.

We need to talk about you and your return

His thumbs moved before his thoughts could stop them.

Who is this

Steve, we need you back u don't belong there

He switched the phone off and then rolled over to turn out his lights. Little sleep came that night.

The next morning started early as Rachel reported for driving duty at the house. As arranged, she had rented a school bus-sized coach for the day's activity.

"Hey, Steve," she said as he entered the home. "We gonna do this."

"Yeah, just gimme a sec," Hyatt said as he downed his third cup of coffee. He longed for the energy drink he envisioned in his future. "Why don't you start loading 'em on?"

"Right." She marched off to comply. Over her shoulder, she called, "Whaddawe gonna do 'bout Roy?"

"Leave Roy to me." He poured a travel cup to take with him. He went to Roy's room.

He found the client rocking in his bed, listening to Leann Rhimes on the headphones to his Walkman. With an indestructible smile plastered to his face, he perseverated on the bed, bouncing to the rhythm of the music as he giggled to her voice. Roy Pena stood five-foot ten weighing over three hundred pounds, most of it from the Mexican food he ate whenever offered. The simplest of Hyatt's charges with an estimated I.Q. below 40, he had entered his care having been grandfathered in. As a client from the seller of the business when Hyatt bought the previous owner out, Roy came with the deal. Otherwise, Hyatt would never agree to take on such an extreme case.

"Come on, Roy. Time to go."

"Wud mo' tong." He held both hands toward Hyatt in a stop fashion.

"No, Roy. No more songs. Let's go."

Without complaint, without even expression, Roy climbed out of the single bed, his Size 12 sneakers on the dirty floor rug Hyatt refused to vacuum. The 'tards had that duty, the cleaning, the rudimentary maintenance, and damned if Hyatt would agree to pick up the slack when they neglected their keep.

"Let's go, buddy." He clapped Roy's shoulder as he passed through the threshold.

At the parking lot of the election poll, a Lutheran church with a mildewed forty-year-old roof, the bus filled with a hundred of the charges, Hyatt turned to Rachel. "So, this is how we run this: you lead them in one at a time, hand them this card –" He showed Rachel a three by five listing the candidates to vote for. "– then wait for them to vote."

"And they know what to do?"

"Yep."

"And they won't –"

"Stop worrying, cuz. We got it covered. They have been trained on exactly what to do."

"And they can read? Follow directions?"

Hyatt's eyes ascended into his eyelids. "All 'cept Roy. I'll monkeysit him while you do this." He shifted in his seat. "Listen, Rachel, stop overthinking it. We been training 'em for years. And you should know better. You was supposed to have a background in this shit. Intelligence has no bearing on the ability to read."

Brockmeyer's voice softened a decibel. "Yeah, right."

"So, no worries. Go to it." He jacked his thumb toward the church. Rachel motioned for William to follow her.

Roy rocked in his bus seat, feet beneath him, listening to "How Do I Live" on his Walkman. Hyatt's phone buzzed. He sighed as he reached into his pocket, dreading the number he knew he'd see. The same caller showed on his screen 666.

He had had enough. Pressing Answer, he barked into the cell, "Who is this?"

An echo sounded in his ear. He heard a distant wind on the line, a cold air blast of winter. Frigid winter.

"Steve, you must return," the voice said. It carried with it the sound of a lost soul, of someone who had already abandoned all hope. Hyatt's skin rippled with goose bumps as he listened to the voice, the sounds coming through as the screams in the distance beyond the voice.

"Who the fuck is this?"

The answer he heard sounded like a cross between "Whoooo" and "Yoooou." If a prank, it surpassed any he had experienced previously.

"Look pal, I ain't playin'. Who the fuck is this?"

The noise he heard on the other end sounded like an ice-driven wind from the Arctic, but colder. A gust of frozen air as millions of mournful souls cried over the horizon. He felt his testicles rise into his groin.

"Return." The voice drifted away as the line went dead.

"What the fuck?" he whispered as he lowered his hand. He saw that all the hairs on his arm now standing on end, his skin feeling as though the temperature had dropped ten degrees.

"Cud ju turd da heatah on, Steve?"

He switched the fan on. "Yeah, no problem." He turned to Roy to see he had drooled all across the front of his tee shirt again. "Roy, use your handkerchief."

He mopped the saliva that had soaked the material of his tee. "Easy- peasy."

"My hair ain't greasy."

Later, as he and Rachel drove the fifth and last busload of voters to their respective houses, Rachel sat behind Hyatt as they headed north on 270. She sat in the shotgun seat behind the driver's seat. Roy, who had been with them the entire time, persevered to "Can't Fight the Moonlight" on his headphones.

"So, help me understand how this works," Brockmeyer said. "What's up with the voting effort among the mentally challenged?"

"You ask a lot of questions, slick. Maybe too many."

"Look, I'm just trying to get a handle on it. You know I ain't got no hidden agenda; I hadda pass a deep, thorough background check before I could work here."

"Yeah, and that's the reason you're still vertical enough to ask all these annoying questions."

"So, give."

"Look, we get paid damn good money to cart around 'tards and to see after 'em. Just take the money and stop asking so many questions."

That evening, as he drifted into a fitful sleep, his phone rang. Groaning, he checked. His ex-wife. He pressed to answer.

"Elizabeth?"

The cold, desolate voice came through. "Steve, if you do not come, we will come after you. A fate you do not want."

He rechecked his screen; it showed the 666 number. "Fuck!"

"Listen, you fuck, you've chosen the wrong guy to fuck with. I don't scare easy, and you can't intimidate me." He held the phone in front of his face, yelling, "Stop calling!"

He spent the rest of the night searching the internet for information on the calls. He checked prank call sites, both how to do them and how to avoid them. He even checked Revelations websites. After all, didn't the number's notoriety come from that book of the bible? He checked information on the telephone companies. How could it be possible that such an Area Code could exist?

As he searched, another text came through.

Steve, you must return

He got no sleep that night.

The next morning, as he had breakfast with his seven charges in the main dining room, he held his head as he drank his coffee. Rachel joined the table.

"Bro, you look like shit."

"Man, I think I'd need to be three days dead to feel better than I do right now."

"No sleep."

"Uh-huh."

"That's tough. What's keeping you up? An actual conscience?"

"Fuck you." He went for his cup. "Lemme ask you a question."

"K."

"You ever hear of calls coming in on phone from an Area Code 666?"

"You mean 666 like –"

"Yeah."

"Like the New Testament –"

"Yeah. Just like that."

Rachel looked at her bowl of Cream of Wheat as if the answer lay within its curdled contents. After a long moment, she said, "Nope, can't say I have." She scooped a spoonful into her mouth.

While they sat, they locked their gazes as a fetid smell overcame them at the table. It reeked of excrement.

"Roy!" Rachel said.

"Roy, I have told you to tell us when you need to poop!" Roy's smile displayed his pride.

"Your turn," Hyatt said.

"No, yours."

They shook their right fists at each other in three motions. Then Rachel displays a fist while Hyatt, his index and middle finger. Hyatt stood to change and clean Roy.

Rachel said, "Easy-peasy."

"Don't act so sleazy."

After delivering the clients to their places of employment, Hyatt drove to the nearest retail outlet for his carrier. Carrying his phone, he stalked the carpeted storefront in the Fallsgrove strip mall. An employee met with him inside a minute.

"How may I help you today?"

"You can help me stop getting all these unwanted fucking calls."

The salesperson, a woman who wore the nametag, Nina, batted her eyes. He realized his transgression.

"Look, I'm sorry. But I've been literally harassed by these continuous calls."

"Have you blocked –"

"Yes."

"And have you –"

"Yes."

"And did you –"

"Yes!"

He raised his hands above his head in frustration. "Nothing works."

"Let's see what we can do."

It turned out to be nothing. Nothing at all.

That afternoon, as he sat in the company van to retrieve the charges from their menial jobs on the assembly line at VidPhone Plus, his phone sprang to life. It rang even though he had switched off the ringer. "Fah-uck." He switched it to speaker phone.

"Who the fuck is this?"

Roy sat in the backseat, rocking while listening to Leann. As progressive as his company was about placing clients in working situations, Roy's reduced intellect prevented even them from finding him employment. A wave of cold entered the interior of the car.

"This is you."

Roy's form, his skin, and hair crystallized into ice, a rock-solid hoarfrost of frozen thickness that covered his face and body like the coating over a garden hose in an overnight snowstorm. Then his features moved, growing tusks as, from within, a deep, broken voice emerged from the cell phone.

"I am you in Hell."

As Roy changed, his skin and body plunging the air to sub-zero temperatures, the phone speaker said, "Steve Hyatt, this is your true form. This is your flesh."

The thing that was Roy reached out to touch him, grabbing his forearm in a clutching grip. Hyatt felt the bone crack as it broke beneath its pressure, the ulna popping through his skin like a plastic straw thrusting through its paper envelope as the fuselage of bone protruded from his muscle. He felt the cold pass through him, his body temperature plummeting to below freezing as ice and frost covered his form.

As he watched, the scene before his eyes melted away as an entire new tableau presented itself. No longer a Maryland DC suburb, he found himself in an ice-layered tundra, a vast stretch of frozen matter where the ground once stood. Out into the horizon, bodies rutted upward from the frozen surface, each covered in frost, all screaming in agony and despair. Likewise, great mountains of glaze loomed in the distance as a bitter wind screamed through the desolation of absolute cold.

The phone speaker spoke, "You see, this is Hell. You are and have been consigned here for six years." He realized he was listening to his voice coming from the phone speaker, his actual voice colored by the electronic audio.

Still gripping his forearm, Roy morphed into Steve Hyatt's form, his own image. Caked in ice like a sleet-soaked snowman, his face looked back at him, the eyes locked in cold, the mouth and lower jaw rigid with hoar.

The speakerphone continued, "You need to understand: I am the real Steven Hyatt. You are merely the demon sent to take my place in the Upper World as I was condemned to Hell for my sin of Treachery to Those to Whom I Have Been Entrusted, a monstrous sin of the most heinous proportions. My time in Hell, in Ptolemaea, was sentenced when you – I – began the evil of this job."

The tibia in his arm broke through the skin to follow its mate, the blood splattering the air, slapping his eyes with wet gore. Unable to move under the grip of the ice-covered thing, he blinked to clear his vision.

He saw the thing's – his – mouth grow, gaping to a degree such that it could swallow a man whole. The thing's neck stretched out to hover above him as the mouth surrounded his head, consuming him in whole as a serpent might swallow an egg. The thing's jaws snapped shut to complete the task.

The scene shifted once more, reverting to Maryland. In the bus, the ice-covered Hyatt spat out the headless body of the decapitated Hyatt, its lifeless form thudding to the metal floor of the vehicle like a burlap sack of rotten fruit.

The thing, the frozen body of Steven Hyatt, its soul now intact, then plodded away, leaving the decapitated body of that which was the demon masquerading as the mortal man to lie in the November air. Its march back to Hell would take a long time. But time it had in eternity.

ERIKA M SZABO
HAUNTING
MEMORIES

As John trudged through the relentless downpour, each step felt like a burden on his exhausted body. The rain pounded against his umbrella with fierce determination, creating a symphony of splashes and echoes that reverberated through the streets. But it wasn't just the clamor that unsettled him; it was the onslaught of memories that flooded back with every drop. Memories of heartache and betrayal as his ex-girlfriend tearfully ended their relationship under the stormy skies. Memories of fear and pain from a harrowing night when he narrowly escaped death in a tragic accident and when his father drove off in the thunderstorm. John never saw him again.

Since he was a young child, each heavy rainfall seemed to unleash a line of disasters, painting the slick streets with shades of sorrow under the hazy glow of streetlights. Every droplet felt like a stab in his heart, dredging up emotions he had long tried to bury beneath the surface.

The bustling city, usually bursting with life and energy, was now draped in a somber cloak. The incessant rain seemed to have washed away all traces of joy, leaving behind a heavy sense of foreboding. As John made his way through the crowded streets, every step felt like a battle against his past. Each drop of rain that fell from the dark clouds above seemed to mirror his swirling emotions and haunting memories. But he persisted, determined to conquer both the physical and emotional challenges posed by the storm. John's mind flickered back to a particularly emotional memory from his elementary school years.

***

It was a long afternoon when he and his mischievous buddies were hunched over their desks serving detention. They were so engrossed in their work that they didn't notice the sun slowly fading behind thick, dark clouds. Suddenly, a distant roar of thunder echoed across the sky, sending shivers down their spines as ominous clouds gathered. The air grew heavy, and a bolt of lightning cracked through the air, signaling the impending storm.

The teacher and students were caught off guard, their minds still occupied with the math problem at hand. But Mother Nature had other plans, unleashing a fury of wind and rain. The students eagerly packed their belongings and rushed out of the classroom, determined

99

to outrun the approaching storm. The first few drops landed on their skin, almost teasingly, before exploding into a relentless downpour. Within minutes, the streets were awash with the sound of heavy rain, drowning out all other noises and creating a hypnotic symphony of water hitting pavement and rooftops.

Navigating through a maze of winding streets and narrow alleys, their feet finally carried them to a park where their paths diverged - each heading toward their homes on opposite sides. John's eyes darted around. Deciding to take a shortcut through the park, he stepped onto the footpath but soon found himself struggling to keep his balance as rain-slicked patches made it treacherous and difficult to progress. The heavy droplets came down with an unrelenting force, soaking his clothes and skin. Despite the obstacles, John pushed forward, determined to get home as fast as he could.

Fueled by a sense of urgency, John braced himself against the relentless onslaught of rain, his arm shielding his face as he pushed forward. With each step, his feet seemed to sink deeper into the muck and mud, making it increasingly difficult to move forward. The rain beat down on him with such ferocity that it penetrated through his clothes, drenching him completely and weighing him down. His hair clung to his scalp in wet, tangled strands. But despite the discomfort and fatigue setting in, he refused to give up or falter. His determination was unwavering, propelling him onward through the storm.

Suddenly, piercing cries shattered the sound of the hollering wind, followed by the sharp report of gunshots. John's heart pounded in his chest as he recognized the unmistakable sounds just a stone's throw away. Without hesitation, he dropped to the ground and pressed himself against the wet vegetation. Through the dense curtain of rain and tangled foliage, he could make out a dark figure hunched over a motionless form on the ground. The only source of light came from sporadic flashes of lightning, casting eerie shadows that danced across the scene before him. Fear and adrenaline coursed through his body as he watched, frozen in place, unsure of what to do next.

John's eyes widened in terror, but he quickly stifled the gasp that threatened to escape his lips. Gripping his teeth tightly, his entire body shook with a potent mix of dread and adrenaline. Despite the overwhelming panic coursing through his body, he forced himself to stay still, determined to observe and make sense of the scene unfolding before him. The looming figure towered over its unmoving victim, casting a dark shadow. John's breath caught in his throat as he watched, unable to tear his gaze away.

A surge of fury contorted the man's features, his face twisted in a mask of rage as he spat out venomous words. "Vermin, like you deserve no less!" His voice was raw and filled with malice. With a swift, brutal kick aimed at the defenseless individual on the ground, he then turned on his heel and hastened away along the path leading toward John's neighborhood. The leaves rustled under his feet, a stark contrast to the violence of his actions. A sense of unease settled over the path as if it could feel the aftermath of his anger lingering in the air.

John's limbs quivered with anguish while he observed the man's retreat, tears clouding his vision as he cautiously rose to his feet. Drawing nearer to the still form, John detected faint grunts, igniting a spark of hope within him. Relief washed over him as he realized the man was alive. The crunching of gravel beneath his shoes reverberated through the eerie surroundings. Kneeling by the wounded stranger, John discerned the steady rhythm of his breathing. Fueled by adrenaline, he leaned closer. The stranger bled profusely from a gash on his forehead; as John hovered beside him, the injured man's eyes fluttered open.

"You're going to be okay," John's words were a lifeline in the dark. "Can you stand?" The man's response was a guttural groan, but with sheer determination, he pushed himself up onto his elbows.

Without hesitation, John peeled off his rain-soaked T-shirt, using it as a makeshift bandage to stop the flow of blood from the man's wound. Crimson droplets seeped through the fabric, creating a macabre pattern against the white material, yet it served its purpose in slowing down the bleeding. With careful precision, John hoisted the injured man upright, bearing his weight as they navigated their way out of the desolate park.

As they emerged from the densely grown trees, John's muscles ached with exhaustion. His wet shoes felt like lead weights, and his breath came in ragged gasps. But as he spotted a police car parked on the street, he mustered up all his remaining strength and approached it. The officer jumped out of the car at the sight of John, offering a helping hand to guide the injured man into the back seat. As they waited for the ambulance, the officer draped a warm blanket over John's shivering body and listened patiently as he recounted the terrifying experience.

The following days were a blur in his memory. He remembered retelling the story countless times, picking out the shooter from a police lineup, but he didn't remember if anyone told him who the injured man was and what happened to him.

***

As John strolled through the park, the vivid recollections of that life-altering night engulfed his thoughts. Because of that experience, he went to law school and became a prosecutor. His goal in life was to clean his neighborhood of crime.

Without warning, his shoe lost traction on the slippery, mud-caked trail, causing him to sway unsteadily. Despite his frantic efforts to steady himself, he careened forward and crashed headlong into a sizable puddle.

The force of the impact jolted a searing pain up John's leg, hinting at a potential broken ankle. As he stood up, the throbbing ache spread through his leg, making it nearly impossible to continue forward. Each movement sent sharp waves of torment shooting through him, causing him to grit his teeth in agony. Despite the pain, he pressed on, determined to get home. With each step, his injured leg protested, causing John to grimace and fight to remain upright. Every stride served as a poignant reminder of his injury as he tentatively advanced, hobbling along with immense struggle. It was as if his body was fighting against itself, wanting to move forward but held back by the intense pain.

With aching muscles and rain-soaked clothes clinging to his skin, John's eyes lit up as he spotted the faint glow of the first streetlamp in the distance. He muttered under his breath, feeling a surge of determination despite the relentless downpour drenching him to the core. Each step forward intensified the throbbing pain in his ankle and foot, but he pressed on, driven by a stubborn resolve.

When he was close to passing out from the pain, he sought refuge beneath a gnarled tree, its branches offering scant protection from the storm. John sank onto the sodden ground. His face twisted in agony as he massaged his swollen foot, trying to alleviate the sharp ache that shot through him. The rain hammered down relentlessly, seeping through his clothes and sending shivers wracking through his body, mingling with feelings of uncertainty and fear.

With grim determination etched on his features, John calculated only 300 yards separating him from his house. "Just a little farther," he whispered to himself through chattering teeth, mustering every ounce of strength to propel himself onward, even if it meant crawling on all fours to reach the front steps.

Lost in contemplation, John's attention was abruptly drawn to a shadowy figure emerging from the relentless downpour. A surge of recognition tickled through him, though the specifics eluded his grasp.

Without time to dwell on this puzzling familiarity, the stranger broke into a welcoming smile as he drew near. "It's me, John. You saved my life back when you were just a boy. Remember? You helped me reach the hospital after I got shot. Let me lend you a hand now, son." John clutched the man's sturdy arm firmly, using it for support as he struggled to bear weight on his injured leg.

Each arduous step demanded his full concentration as he willed himself onward. The man remained resolute but wordless, his expression conveying unwavering determination as he guided John up the stairs toward the front door.

As they approached the entrance, John's weight sagged against the railing, and with trembling fingers, he pressed the doorbell, his chest expanding with a mix of gratitude and relief. The door creaked open at a leisurely pace, prompting John to spin around to face his rescuer, eager to convey his heartfelt thanks. Yet, much to his bewilderment, the man had vanished. Grateful yet puzzled by this mysterious turn of events, John stood there in silence.

His mother hurried to the door lobby, ushering him inside and guiding him toward the waiting elevator. Once they were safely in their apartment, she tended to his swollen ankle, applying a makeshift ice pack.

At that moment, a flood of memories cascaded through John's mind like an unstoppable tide. Recollections of the night he aided the injured man flooded back to him, and it dawned on him that this very individual was now repaying the favor by helping him home.

John sat at the kitchen table, his eyes fixed on his mother as he carefully broached the subject that had been repressed in his mind for all those years. "Mom, do you remember the man from Baker Street who was shot when I was in fourth grade?"

Her face softened with recollection as she nodded, her eyes reflecting a mix of sorrow and gratitude. "Yes, I remember Mr. Jones well," she replied softly. "He was a brave soul who changed our neighborhood for the better."

Intrigued, John leaned in closer, eager to learn more about the mysterious figure who had left such a lasting impact. "What happened to him?"

His mother's gaze turned somber as she began to unravel the tale of Mr. Jones' heroism. "He was an unsung hero, a police informant who risked everything to rid our streets of gangs," she explained. "Thanks to his courage, our community is safer now."

John listened intently, feeling a sense of admiration welling up within him for the man he had unknowingly crossed paths with. A flicker of recognition sparked in John's eyes as he connected the dots. "I knew I recognized him," he mused with a hint of a smile tugging at his lips. Determination flashed in his gaze as he made a silent vow to repay Mr. Jones for his selfless actions once he had recovered from his injury. "He just helped me to get home."

The air grew heavy with an unexpected revelation as his mother's demeanor suddenly shifted. "That can't be," she whispered hoarsely, her voice barely audible. "He passed away in a tragic accident four years ago."

A wave of disbelief washed over John as her words hung in the air.

HE WATCHES
DAVID W. THOMPSON

*H*e crouched in the shadows, a creature of the night—a purveyor of passion and a despoiler of dreams. He was young—or young for what he was—ancient in human terms. After a century of watching over three mortal generations, he was well acquainted with waiting ...but he finally found her. She was born, became a woman, and his time was at hand. Their time! His tongue slid over darkened lips. A dribble of saliva, stained red from his evening meal, framed his smile. As patient as any alpha predator, he watched and waited.*

***

Evelyn Barrow sighed as she gazed at the old, framed image in her lap. It was an old black-and-white photo, faded by time and handling. Her father passed it down to her through his father, who first received it from his mother—Eve's great-grandmother, one of the figures in the picture. Alexandra Perkins had been the only female in her family line for generations—until Evelyn was born.

Her father said the picture was from the World War II era. The man in the picture, dressed in an old-style Army uniform, lent credence to his story. Evelyn's research identified the outfit as a paratrooper's garb. Her family's oral tradition said the man was killed in action in the liberation of the Dachau prison camp. After surviving the horrors of the war, he was killed when his parachute failed to open.

The photo's edges were dogeared, and several creases marred its surface. The blurred focus was the product of an amateur photographer, but somehow, the feelings of the two people were evident. They were in love.

A bent-backed elderly lady in a red plaid apron entered the sitting room with a feather duster in her hand.

"Do you need for anything, Miss Perkins...I mean, Mrs. Barrow?" she asked.

"Iris, after all the years you've been with our family, couldn't you please call me Evelyn or Eve?"

"Yes. Misses...umm, I mean—Evelyn."

"Please, put that down and sit with me for a moment."

Iris sat on the sofa beside her, keeping a respectful distance.

106

"What do you know about this picture, Iris? And the man in it with my great-grandmother?"

"Surely, you've heard the stories, child? I was told he was in love with your great-grandmother and died in the war."

"Were they? In love, I mean? What do you remember?"

"How old do you think I am, Miss?"

"I meant no offense, Iris. They look so happy..." Evelyn dropped her face into her hands and sobbed. Iris put an arm around her, stiffly at first, then tenderly—as if she were her child.

"There, there, Evelyn. Don't carry on so. Married life takes some adjustment. You love Mister Barrow, and he loves you. Love conquers all, as my mother used to say."

"I'm not so sure." Evelyn sniffed and turned her head onto the older woman's shoulder, wetting her dress with tears.

"I'll tell you a secret about that picture if it will cheer you up, child, but first, you must dry your tears."

Nodding her head, Evelyn swabbed at her eyes with the tissue Itris held. "I'm sorry, Iris. I am acting like a child. Forgive me?"

"There's nothing to forgive, Evelyn." Iris stood and picked up her feather duster.

"Wait, Iris. I still want to hear that story you promised," she patted the cushion beside her.

"Are you sure?" Iris asked, and Evelyn nodded. "Do you believe in ghosts, Evelyn?"

"I'm not sure. I've never seen one, but Daddy swore he did once. He was convinced it was the spirit of his grandfather."

"Well, your father didn't know this story. His father kept it from him. He was a grand old southern gentleman, your grandfather, but he didn't truck in ghosts and things that go bump in the night. He said there were enough worrisome things in this life without borrowing trouble."

"I don't remember my grandfather very well, but that sounds right."

"I believe the man who died at Dachau concerned him, though. He said such great evil festers, spreads, and draws in even darker things, wicked things born of ancient evil. Evelyn, that man—the one in the picture? Your grandfather said his mother saw that man several times—years after he died, mind you. He said she thought good things happened to her and your family whenever she saw him. She called him her guardian angel because she'd see him, especially when times were hard, and they'd get better."

"What kinds of things?"

"Dreams and prayers made real. Promotions, land bought for pennies on the dollar and sold for double its worth, getting out of the stock market before the crash. With every appearance, your family's wealth and standing increased.

"It happened in your grandfather's time too, although he'd never admit it, but housekeepers hear things. When the Watcher visited your grandfather, I heard them talking— well, your grandfather, anyway. I only heard his responses to unheard questions. The walls in the old house were thin, and Mr. Perkins was never a quiet man."

"What did the man—the Watcher, want, do you think?"

"My best guess? The same as any man. He wanted a woman—a particular woman."

***

John Barrow woke from a deep, dreamless sleep. He listened for any sound that might have disturbed him, but there was only the soft intake of breath from his sleeping wife, Eve. He raised his head from his down-filled pillow and tossed aside the 1000-thread-count Egyptian cotton sheets. Slipping his feet into new Prada leather slippers, he rolled from the bed and stepped toward the arched bedroom window.

At the sound of shattering glass, Evelyn Barrow bolted upright and screamed. She raced to the destroyed window and touched the drop of deep red blood on the broken glass frame. She looked down at the well-tended flower beds two stories below. They were undisturbed.

"John!" she yelled.

108

Above, the shrouded moon moved in and out of the misty charcoal-black clouds. It was full and as orange as a Halloween jack-o-lantern, a sight that sent shivers down Evelyn's spine. For a moment, it held her mesmerized. The pockmarked façade seemed more demonic than the man-on-the-moon description of her youth. *Bloated with pestilence.* That was how her witchy Great-Aunt Bess described such a moon—one promising impending doom for the viewer.

"John, where are you?"

She slipped on the cashmere robe John bought for her birthday and ran out of the door barefoot.

"John? Are you OK?"

As Evelyn reached the first-floor landing, a white bob of hair peeked out from the edge of a partially opened door.

"Whatever is it, Mrs. Barrow? What's happened?"

"The window was shattered in our room, Iris —there's blood and John…I don't know what's happened to John."

"I'm sure it is nothing, Miss. Probably a branch in the wind on this horrid night and red sap from the tree. I've asked Mr. Barrow if our man should come out and trim back that old oak. But let me check his study. You know Mr. Barrow often enjoys a nightcap in the wee hours."

***

John Barrow woke from his fitful and nightmarish sleep. His back was cramped, and he swiped at something tickling his well-defined jawline. He rolled to his side. There were flashing red and blue lights below him. *I'm dreaming*, he thought. *I certainly didn't fall asleep in the crotch of the old oak.* He laughed at the insanity of his dream and reached for the comfort of his wife's breast—and grasped only air! A hand that smelled of death and sour dirt muffled his scream. John recoiled and slipped from his perch. Another hand snatched his arm in a painful grip before he plummeted to his death. John turned to face the man (or his dream?).

The pale creature raised one eyebrow. Its pupils glowed red in the moonlight.

"Who are you? What are you?" John asked.

"I'm known by many names. My given name, when I was like you, was Alistair. The few who know me today—and still live to address me, call me Corwyn. I like that name. It means 'heart's friend,' Who's better suited than I to claim such a title? Who has done more in matters of the heart? Yes, you may call me Corwyn for the duration of our acquaintance."

The creature smiled a wide, toothsome smile. Needle-sharp incisors, long as a wolf's, glistened in the darkness.

"Wha—what are you? What do you want?"

"Oh? Have I not explained that to your satisfaction, John? I am here for love. I am here for Evelyn—she is destined to be mine. I've seen how you treat my beloved and the results of your union. I've watched and waited for her. You don't mind, do you, John?"

"Yes, I do mind."

"It was a rhetorical question, you hairless whimpering ape."

"I've treated Evelyn well! She has the best of everything that money can buy."

"Indeed, you have, John. Everything money could buy…her money, that is!"

"How do you know…"

"You don't deserve her, John. She is meant for me."

John swung a roundhouse blow that did not connect, and sharp bayonet-like claws dug deep into his neck.

***

Evelyn closed the door as the last deputy left her house. Tears flowed down her cheeks after the hours of questioning and accusations. None that led to any answers concerning the whereabouts of her husband.

"Iris—this 'Watcher' you spoke of? I think I've seen him, and I'm scared. Maybe he, or it, is what has disturbed my sleep so many nights. Could he have taken John? I have dreamt of such a man since I was a little girl. I thought it was because I was drawn to that photo. It

110

used to be once or twice a year, but it's been almost every night since I got engaged."

"Dreams can seem real, Evelyn. Nightmares even more so."

"It seems real when he shows up. And it's never a nightmare. I always considered him a figment of my overactive imagination, a perfect man I dreamed up for myself. He is always considerate and gentle in my dreams."

"The devil wears many masks, Evelyn. He wants us to believe he is an ugly, horned monster. He can appear as whatever we yearn for."

"Iris, are you suggesting that I've been seduced in my dreams for years by a ghost, or worse, a demon? It can't be. I pray. I believe in the Creator by whatever name She is called. I try to be righteous and spiritual, even if not religious."

"I mean no disrespect, Mrs. Barrow; my apologies."

"Apologies? Iris, I feel like I am the worst kind of disloyal wife. What if this 'Watcher' did do something to John? That's all I've been able to think of since the deputies arrived. They already think I did something to my husband anyway. But if the ghost or demon is real— did I do something to encourage him?"

"Don't get ahead of yourself, Evelyn. For all we know, John stepped out to have a beer at O'Donnel's Pub. The deputies said the same. But if something happened to John, you are not responsible. If anyone hurt him, they are responsible. It's their evil, their guilt, not yours."

"He's not answering his cell phone, but he always has it. Something has happened. I feel it in my bones."

***

John stirred and fearful of waking to the same nightmare, opened his eyes to narrow slits. He was bound and gagged. A noose was tied loosely around his neck, daring him to fall.

"Ah, the sleeping wannabe prince wakes. Did my kiss draw you from your slumbers, sweet prince?"

At the sound of the creature's voice, blood flowed from the gaping slash in John's neck. The thing named Corwyn dropped his

111

head and suckled. John recoiled in horror until his eyes glossed over, and he smiled in ecstasy. Corwyn lifted his head, licked his lips, and smiled.

"Only a mother with heavy breasts can appreciate how hunger's call draws forth nourishment. The donor knows joy despite the pain. Is it not so?"

"Stay away from me. What are you?"

"I gather that my words do not suffice, my dim-witted friend. Perhaps it best if I show you."

Corwyn touched John's forehead with a cold, clawed hand. John's vision blurred, and when it refocused, he no longer looked out upon Society Row.

He saw two children, a boy and a girl—perhaps nine or ten years old. They were playing tag on a well-kept lawn. The boy was the faster of the two, and when he tagged the raven-haired girl, she tripped and fell forward. The boy slid down beside her and wiped her tears. He looked at her as tears formed in his eyes. He leaned forward and kissed her scraped knee.

Through Corwyn's ears, John heard a door slam and an irritated woman's voice.

"Alexandra, you come in here this instant. As for you, young man, stay away from my daughter! We don't want your kind here."

Another whirling, blurry spell and a couple appeared reclining on a blanket at an unknown beach. Feeling like a voyeur, John watched as they shared a meal. The man, who looked like a more human version of Corwyn (Alistair?), leaned into the woman and kissed her. She returned his embrace, stood, and raced away from her suitor. When her face came into view, John gasped.

It was Evelyn! If not her, indeed her twin. But it couldn't be! And her swimming suit looked like a contraption from the Middle Ages— but it was her face.

His vision blurred again, and he found himself at a train station. The same man and woman were there. The man, now dressed in an old-style Army uniform, held the woman close.

"I will come back to you, Alexandra."

"I'm afraid for you, Alistair. What if…What if you're…"

"Killed? Even death would not destroy our love. I will return."

Blurring away then until the next images appeared, a kaleidoscope of scenes. Alistair, in boot camp, is harassed by drill sergeants. Bloody battles and tortured bodies followed repeated jumps from aircraft. The finale as Alistair pulled at his ripcord, but his chute refused to open. John felt the freefall, the wind in his face, and the terror as he hurtled to his, or rather Alistair's, death. The impact was felt in his bones. John screamed in agony. Something dark and fast— so fast. It was a shadow, a distortion racing toward him. A gaping mouth full of predacious teeth…a searing pain in his neck. John smiled as his…no, as Alistair's life slipped away in ecstasy.

Corwyn removed his hand, and John's vision was his own again.

"When I returned to my beloved Alexandra, it was many years later. To the new me, Corwyn, it seemed like days. My master, my maker, kept me ignorant of her and what I was. But that is of no significance to my tale. When we next met, Alexandra was a middle-aged woman as beautiful as the day we parted. But she'd married another. They had a child and a grandchild in my absence. Her faith in our love was not strong enough. She did not trust my resolve."

"What did you expect? You died! And what could you know of love?" *Am I really arguing with a creature in a dream?* "Whatever you once were, Corwyn, you became a monster, a merchant of death."

"Alexandra also named me monster until I proved myself to her again…until she knew the depths of my love."

"She rejected you, nonetheless. She died before Evelyn was a spark in her father's eye. What right do you have to lay any claim upon my wife?"

"Rejected? No. Alexandra swore eternal love, but she'd made a family and felt our time past—but never our love. She promised to return to me as I had to her. 'Watch my bloodline,' she said, 'and we will meet again. Our love will be renewed.'"

John laughed. "So, you believe Evelyn is the reincarnation of your lost love, Alexandra? You are a fool if you do, or that Evelyn could ever love you, a monster."

"And you, John? I've watched you. Are you less of a monster than I? Living off the wealth and advantage you never earned? Elevating yourself above men who earn their living by the sweat of their brow? Looking down on them when the reverse would be truer. What has Evelyn gained from your love besides heartache and a diminished bank account? You are a user and a worm, John Barrow."

"She loves me."

"See what tragedy your love will bring."

Again, Corwyn placed his hand on John's brow. But it wasn't Corwyn's past he saw, but rather his and Evelyn's future.

***

Evelyn tossed about in her bed—their bed. Sleep never came easy for her, but now it was impossible.

What had happened to John? Where was he, and was he OK? Was he in trouble? Did she drive him away? Did he need her now? Did the mysterious Watcher grab him from their bed and spirit him away? Was the Watcher real? Or did some other dirty secret or unknown enemy from her family's past harm him?

The questions were many; the answers were few. After a week, the Sheriff's department seemed to have forgotten about him. One deputy told her, in confidence, that they thought John staged his disappearance. There were no ransom demands. Besides the thin smear of blood on the broken windowpane, there were no other signs of foul play. John had disappeared like a thief in the night. The broken window, covered now with a taped-on plastic sheet, was a daily reminder.

She peered through the plastic toward the stately oak. Something about it unsettled her. *Did something move along its trunk?* She must remind Iris to call her man about trimming it up. The branches threatened to rip open the plastic every night.

Did John know she loved him? Their silly fight the night he disappeared seemed an eternity ago. Evelyn forgot for a moment what the fight was about. It seemed insignificant now, but was it the straw that broke the camel's back? Did her sharp words drive John away? Even Iris overheard her berating John for his extravagant spending. Most of what he spent was on her, but was that even the root cause of

114

the argument? Wasn't it just as much about the attractive woman he spoke to at The Catalina restaurant that night?

When Evelyn returned from the Lady's Room that evening, the woman was bent over John, whispering in his ear. She had an incredible body, with waves of auburn hair reaching her waist. The woman laughed often and with ease. Small talk and flirting seemed second nature to her—skills Evelyn had never acquired. She hated her and wanted to be like her at the same time.

Evelyn was at the table before the woman could make a graceful exit, and introductions were unavoidable.

"Suzanne Richter, this is my wife, Evelyn Barrow. Evelyn— Suzanne." The woman nodded and smiled, then slipped away as their meals arrived.

On the way home, Evelyn's curiosity and jealousy overwhelmed her.

"How do you know that woman, John?"

"What woman?"

"Suzanne- Something or other…"

"Richter. She is an old family friend."

"Did you have a relationship with her?"

John shook his head and furrowed his brow. "Why would that matter, Eve? You are my wife. It's you I love."

"John?"

"Evelyn, she was my mother's nurse from hospice. It isn't a time I like to remember or talk about."

***

The visions Corwyn evoked painted a bleak picture of John and Evelyn's future. John saw their bitter fights over the silliest things, the years filled with Evelyn's tears. A child was born—a boy, John Jr. The lad didn't live to his first birthday. Evelyn cried in her grief, broken in spirit yet struggled on. John turned to the bottle, and Evelyn cried even more. Another woman entered the picture, and John was smitten. On the eve of their tenth anniversary, John watched as Evelyn sat in her bath—and slit her wrists…

115

"No!" John shouted and pushed away the creature's hand. "Liar! Why are you showing me these sick lies?"

"I've only shown you the truth. I'm many things, but I am never a liar. That's your future and Evelyn's demise."

"Can the future be changed? Is there something I can do?"

"Unlikely. As much chance as a leopard changing his spots."

"Then kill me."

"What?"

John swung his legs from the tree branch and slipped off his perch.

Corwyn snatched John's wrist with one hand and pulled him back up.

"Fool, you'd die for her?" Corwyn asked. His mouth gaped open like a snake devouring its prey and feasted on John's blood. At the creature's touch, John smiled. When the light began to dim in John's eyes, Corwyn pulled away.

"Not yet, little ape. The fun has only begun."

***

Evelyn rubbed the sleep from her eyes and ran to the bedroom door.

"Iris? Are you all right? I thought I heard something." There was no response from below but a ripping sound behind her. She turned back into her room. As she watched, a sliver of moonlight slipped through the plastic at the window and grew. *Something was ripping through the plastic!*

As the slit grew, an arm pushed its way through, followed by a pasty white face that struck fear in her heart.

"No! Iris, help. There's an intruder!"

The man held a finger to his lips, and Evelyn felt a strange peace settle over her.

"Who are you?" she asked as he cleared the windowsill.

116

"Don't you recognize me, Alexandra—uh, Evelyn? Not even from your dreams? We've spent many evenings conversing. You've asked me in…"

"I remember you. Are you the Watcher?"

Corwyn offered a half-smile and bowed. "Please call me Corwyn. I've searched for many years to find you. I've watched, as you say, and I've waited. I've wanted nothing more or less than you for an eternity."

"No! You don't know me. You are a—shade—a phantasm of my dreams."

"I know you better than anyone, Eve."

"Why are you here? What do you want?"

"I am here for love. I am here for you, sweet Evelyn. You've been the promise I've held near my heart since before you were born. Come away with me, and I'll show you all the happiness the world has to offer. I'll cover you with riches, give you the gift of eternal life, and love you with all I am forever."

"Corwyn, I've dreamt of you often. I even yearned for you in lonely moments, but it's too late. If you've watched, as you say, you know I love another. My husband John is…"

"Is undeserving of you. He will be the death of you."

"No, we love each other."

"I'll show you." Corwyn reached out and placed his palm on her cheek. The vision he'd shared with John appeared before her eyes. When it was done, Corwyn took his hand away. Evelyn's tears flowed like water in a mountain stream.

"Now, I would show you our life together."

He reached out to touch her again. Evelyn pushed his hand away.

"I don't need to see it, Corwyn."

"Then you are ready to join me? To rekindle our love? I'll make you so happy." He bared his teeth and paused at the nape of her neck, drawing in her scent.

***

117

Corwyn jumped from the hastily patched window and glided to the ground. A dark figure slipped out from the shadows.

"Did the woman fulfill your desires, Corwyn?"

"Master? You followed me here?"

"I feel like a father to you, Corwyn. How could I not? Is it as I said? That their kind cannot accept us?"

"No. It is far worse. Human prejudice would be far kinder."

"Love is not for the likes of us, Corwyn."

"She is all I've wanted since I was a suckling at my mother's breasts and well before you turned me, master. She is the only reason I live. The only way I can endure the horrors I've committed. But their love is also true. They'd die for one another! I must win her over. It is our destiny."

"Did you show her the future? With him? With you?"

"I showed her the death that awaits her with him, but she wouldn't see more. 'Love will find a way,' she said."

"You would leave now if ever you loved her."

"But...our destiny..."

"Destiny is an aggrandized term for vague and arrogant dreams. Love is a word struggling to encompass a primal life force and failing miserably. You are Corwyn—heart's friend. They would die for each other—for the love they share. What measure is your destiny against that?"

"But..."

The ancient creature bared his fangs. "It is All Hallow's Eve, Corwyn, and we can walk among them and take our pick. Come celebrate the night and leave this fantasy behind."

"I haven't the stomach for it, Master. I..."

"Enough--rip her from her life and her love then or feast upon her flesh and blood. One is no more merciful than the other. Look in your heart, Corwyn. Or be a fool and a hypocrite. I am done with you."

The master spread his arms and disappeared into the night. Corwyn hung his head and sulked in the shadow of the old oak.

***

John Barrow woke from a deep, troubled sleep on a pillow dampened by his drool. He listened for any sound that might have disturbed him, but there was only the soft intake of breath from his sleeping wife, Eve. She'd never believe the nightmare he'd had but thought it better if he spared her the details. It seemed so real. He touched a sore spot on his neck and wondered...No. Still, John knew he'd become a better man, a better husband because of it.

He rolled over to spoon into Evelyn and felt a cool breeze. *Why hadn't he noticed the broken window? He'd ask Iris to have her man fix it in the morning.*

***

Corwyn ran with the speed attributed to his kind until far away from Society Row. Far away from Evelyn/Alexandra and his ill-fated destiny.

Before dawn, he stopped on a hill in the center of a 500-acre field, then sat and waited for the new day. He smiled as the first rays of the sun peaked above the distant trees. At the sun's first harsh kiss, his flesh blistered and popped. His hair crisped to cinders in the following minutes, which seemed like hours. The black blood coursing through his veins began to boil. He knew an agony he'd never felt before—and finally understood the power of love.

As his dark soul fled his body, a primal scream echoed across the valley.

***

All Saint's Day dawned with John and Evelyn sitting on their front porch, sipping coffee. When the scream reached them across the miles, John jumped up from his chair.

"Oh, dear God. What was that?"

Evelyn dabbed her eyes at the sound, and a mirthless smile tugged the edge of her lips.

"Some poor creature's life is done, John. It is the death knell of an immortal love."

119

THE LAST
RESORT
SHEBAT LEGION

On a day unlike any other day, Rose walked into the airport. Her sneakers made minimal sound as she pulled her only suitcase behind her on its almost soundless wheels. Rose glanced up, her face wooden, looking for the correct terminal number.

Her face was expressionless as she walked through the metal detector arch without glancing at the man who waved her through.

Rose walked toward the last barrier, her passport clutched in her hand.

"Destination?"

"Mexico," Rose answered, "for the festival."

"Los dia Mortes?"

"Yes," Rose tonelessly affirmed.

"Where are you staying, and for how long?"

Rose mentioned the resort, adding, "Ten days."

The woman gave a double-take and returned Rose her ticket and passport without further conversation. She only motioned her through the gate and pointed to the small lounge where several people sat quietly, with their carry-ons waiting to board.

Rose chose to stand at the window, where she numbly watched as the airplane taxied into place and the bridge was driven toward the plane door and readied.

Rose gave a polite, distant nod to the flight attendant who helped her find her seat during boarding, then stared through the plane's window, ignoring the woman beside her; she hadn't expected it. The aircraft had few passengers, and Rose had looked forward to not having to climb over someone to get to the aisle, let alone fend off a conversation.

"Is this your first time in Mexico?"

Rose bit her lip in annoyance, answering curtly, "Yes."

"Ah, not for me," the woman gave a laugh, "I go away, I come back."

Rose gave a noncommittal grunt.

A flight attendant stopped, offering a pre-flight beverage, but Rose shook her head, only to have the woman scold her, "You go without too much, I think. You must have juice for a toast if you will not have something stronger."

Rose looked at the woman's determined face and shrugged at the attendant, who nodded in affirmation before leaving to take other orders.

"Better, but not by much, eh?"

Rose looked at the woman again, who gave a broad smile on a face creased with deep lines—an older woman wearing a dark, shapeless dress and wrapped in a shawl. On her lap, she held a large purse, into which she reached, searching, smacked her lips with satisfaction, and offered Rose a granola bar.

"Eat," she urged the reluctant Rose, "you are thin, yes? Too much. And not by wanting to be thin, I think? Yes?"

The woman pushed the bar into Rose's hand and took it without further argument. And, when her juice arrived, Rose took it because it didn't matter; it just didn't matter anymore.

"A toast, yes?"

Rose shrugged.

"To those we love and all who have loved us, we drink this in memory."

Rose ignored the toast and the safety demonstration and put on her seatbelt when the indicator lights came on. The plane taxied into position, and she closed her eyes as she felt it accelerate beneath her, feeling herself pushed back into the seat as the aircraft angled up toward the clouds.

"Do not fear, no, not at all," the woman said.

"I am not afraid," Rose retorted grimly, then added as a polite afterthought, "but thank you."

"It is okay to be afraid," the woman said, "sometimes."

Rose did not reply and continued looking out of the window as the woman beside her began to hum to herself.

"Fear is good, eh? Sometimes, eh? It is a good teacher," the woman chuckled.

Rose gave the woman a sidelong look but didn't respond.

The woman patted Rose's hand. "Grief, and her sister, Mourning. They accept offerings of tears as their due, but they do not demand them forever."

"What are you talking about," Rose demanded. "You are talking foolishness."

"Am I? Maybe, maybe," the woman cackled. "But even so, it is true."

Rose grunted in annoyance, glaring at the woman who only smiled at her with sympathy before adding softly, "Depression is a woman; she is a demon, that one; her hair hangs like a greasy shroud, covering eyes as black as the blackest night."

Rose's eyes widened in alarm as the woman took her hand firmly, in her own, and attempted to free herself to no avail.

"Yes, her hair, hanging like a shroud," the woman repeated," and her arms are thin, and her hands, they grab you, eh? They pull you close to her breast, which hides a heart that does not beat."

"Who are you?" Rose whispered, "I will scream. I will."

"She presses her cold lips to yours," the woman continued earnestly, "until your breath is gone, and your soul cries, but it is trapped in a frozen shell."

"Stop it, stop it, "Rose whimpered.

"She clings to you, no matter how far you run or where. Your tears turn into a lake of oil, and you sink beneath like a stone, and …"

"What," Rose whispered.

"Well, you drown, girl, you drown."

Rose felt the onset of tears, a snake around her throat that constricted tighter until tears slid down her cheek no matter how hard she fought.

The woman clapped her hands suddenly, "sleep!"

And Rose dreamed.

They ran on four legs, ears streamed behind. The crisp air whistled through their nose, and they could smell everything. There was no before or after; there was only now, and in the now, they ran, and it was joyous.

A sound, a name, his name, she was calling him, and he ran happily at the sound of her voice. There were no words, only images and feelings of love, safety, food, fun, home, and always and only her, and she ran with him into her embrace. They were together, and it was now, and it was then, and it was forever, and he was in her lap, her giant dog that was that was so small, so, so small.

And in the dream, Rose was happy.

The plane shuddered, and Rose woke with a smile on her face. She turned to the woman beside her, but she was not there, nor did she return as the plane landed, screeching onto the runway. Rose grabbed her bag, exited the aircraft, and entered the sudden night, looking for the shuttle to her resort.

"El Día de los Muertos," the woman whispered, and Rose gave a start. "According to tradition, the gates of heaven open at midnight on October 31, and the spirits of children can rejoin their families for 24 hours." The woman patted Rose on the cheek. "And he was like your child, yes?"

Rose nodded, eyes brimming with tears.

"You bring an offering for the ofrendas, the altar?"

Rose nodded again, choking back sobs, reaching into her bag and taking out a photograph.

The woman looked at the photo, "it is a good likeness, no?"

Rose looked at the picture of her dog and whispered, "Yes, it was a good day."

"A good day lasts forever, my dear, never lost, never."

As a tear slid down Rose's face onto the photograph, she stood suddenly before an altar lit by a thousand candles. Gentle hands guided her, and Rose placed the photo gently on a lighted shelf, only to see the image had changed.

Rose stared at a picture of herself.

She backed up in sudden fear but felt the comforting nose of her dog pushing at her hand, and she fell to her knees, wrapping her arms around him, her face buried into his fur.

"Forever," the woman said from somewhere in the darkness, and a thousand and more voices echoed the word.

"Forever."

Rose walked, her beloved dog by her side, into the night, and the candles flickered, then died, one by one, behind her.

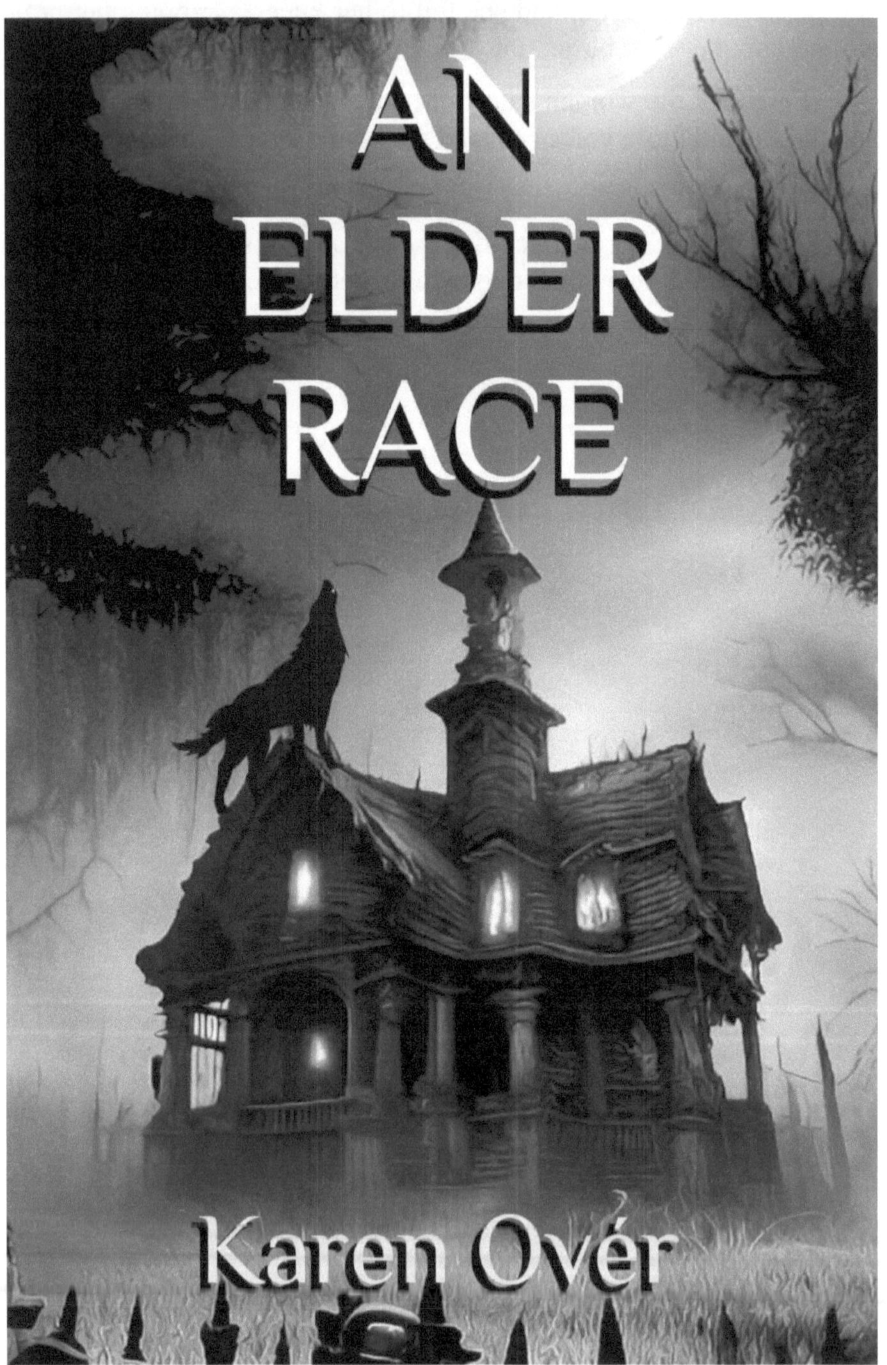
AN
ELDER
RACE
Karen Ovér

Leon Birch sat inside his rented room, listening to the Senate committee hearings. Eating his cold supper, wishing he could afford to get married. Since getting his degree, he'd only been able to pick up a few substitute teaching jobs.

Listening to the government root out subversives usually gave him hope for the future, but now it all seemed far away. The hearings were all taking place back east, and he was in San Francisco, which seemed to be ground zero for everything that was going wrong these days.

It really wasn't fair that he was living alone, paycheck to paycheck. He had all the skills and all the credentials. He certainly had the necessary moral convictions, yet the good jobs all seemed to be taken by determined spinsters and others of questionable politics and even more questionable "lifestyles." No wonder the public schools were turning out delinquents.

And worse, like that Carstairs boy in the fifth-grade class he'd taught today. To Leon's great annoyance, the school he'd graced with his services was one of those careless places that allowed the students to wear costumes on Halloween. Leon wasn't having that nonsense and required his class to remove their dime store covers and masks. All would have been well but for the Carstairs boy.

Instead of a cheap costume thrown over his school clothes, Patrick Carstairs was dressed in green and brown, with some sort of ivy twined around his tattered sweater. The same stuff was also tangled in his black hair, which Leon thought badly needed cutting. Instead of a mask, the boy wore makeup. Not only eyeliner but glitter, for heaven's sake.

"What are you supposed to be, young man?"

"Robin Goodfellow, sir," was the grinning imp's answer.

Leon glanced down to scan the attendance chart. The class tittered, so he changed his gaze to the seating chart and found the impertinent brat's name. "I don't know how you got out of the house dressed like that, Carstairs, but it won't do. Go to the restroom, wash that filth from your face, get rid of that shrubbery, and comb your hair."

The whole class stared in dumbfounded silence. "What are you waiting for, Carstairs? Get on, and don't be all day about it!"

As the boy slunk toward the door, something else caught Leon's eye. "What on earth is *this*?" He yanked at the boy's ear, and a pointed rubber tip came off in his hand. "*Fairy* ears?" Leon pulled the other ear tip off and threw them in the wastebasket. "Your parents shall hear of this. Now get going."

The class kept their heads right down after that, working away on the assignment he gave them. Should have been a simple task to fill their day, writing a family history. But again, the Carstairs boy proved a problem.

"We come from an Elder Race. My grandfather, Jonathan Hamilton Carstairs, came to San Francisco in 1912. He established Carstairs House on top of Shipwreck Hill because the hill is full of faerie magic, just like the place he came from, the Hamilton estate in England, called Oakwood. Oakwood is named for its ancient oak groves. Some of the trees are harvested, but some are left untouched so our Faerie ancestors can continue their revels, and the Carstairs family retains the blessing of the Fair Folk. Carstairs House doesn't have oak trees, but Uncle Nigel planted a holly hedge all around the property to contain the magic. So, our house has the blessing of our High King Oberon and our High Queen Titania, and the Fair Folk are free to hold their revels in our secret garden at the center of the holly maze.

"Halloween is a special night for the Fair Folk. They often reveal themselves to mortals during the hours when the veil between the faerie and mortal realms is thinnest. Especially the Huntsman. He is King Oberon's enforcer. Unlike the courtly knights who are defenders of the faerie realm, the Huntsman is a monster. Darker than night, but for his eyes, which shine red with lust for the blood the Wild Hunt demands. He leads a pack of damned souls in pursuit of other damned souls, who will, in turn, join his Wild Hunt. Unless the High King has decreed they be hunted to death, in which case, the Wild Hunt shows no mercy. Even their horses will join the hounds in rending the prey till nothing remains."

Leon smiled, recalling his enjoyment of the shock on the boy's face when he handed back the paper at the end of the day with a large red F in the upper margin.

"I'll be speaking to your parents about this, Carstairs."

"So will I, Mr. Birch," the imp replied, pouting.

And just before the brat ran from the classroom, he dug into the wastebasket to retrieve the pointed ear tips.

The news ended, and Leon switched off the radio. The more he thought about it, the more he wanted to speak to Mr. and Mrs. Carstairs tonight. No doubt the brat had retrieved the ears because he'd stashed the rest of his costume somewhere and meant to paint himself up like a degenerate again before meeting up with other little hoodlums to terrorize the neighborhood. He certainly didn't trust the little monster to have told them what happened or shown them his schoolwork.

Going out would be annoying, with the streets full of Halloween hooligans. He might even run into the Carstairs boy. He'd just have to take his chances. Anything was better than sitting in a dark, silent room to avoid the incessant demands for candy.

Setting off through the fog, he was quickly disconcerted, for the light of the full moon reflected off the mist, shrouding everything in a silver blanket. When the lights of a small market loomed up, Leon asked for directions.

"Excuse me, can you tell me how to find One Shipwreck Hill?"

"Carstairs House? Right up there at the top of the hill. Just follow the lights." The shopkeeper, a gnarled old man with a guttural foreign accent, appeared to be dressed as The Hunchback. Or perhaps he actually was. Leon didn't want a closer look, but he got one anyway as the man leaned in, laughing at him.

"Watch yerself up there, mister! Strange things happen up there on nights such as this!"

Leon backed away quickly. Was the whole city mad for this loathsome tradition? "Well, I'm not putting up with it, and whatever is in that house up there is getting a piece of my mind."

Leon set his eyes on the flickering jack o' lanterns lining the winding drive and trudged upward through the fog. Tall gates closed off the driveway, though he could see cars parked by the dimly lit house. Angered, he gave the gates a shove. One creaked open just enough to let him squeeze through, then banged shut so fast he jumped.

Oddly, the fog felt thicker here at the top of the hill. Leon followed the leering jack o' lanterns up the drive, through a large open garage into some sort of porch, then out into a back garden. Here, the jack o' lanterns gave way to torches, as if he'd stepped out of 1957 San Francisco and into some ancient realm. He remembered what the boy had written.

We come from an Elder Race.

Windswept clouds covered the moon, and the fog swirled around Leon, making him shiver. Following the line of torches, he stumbled a bit, stepping down through the terraced gardens. Seeing someone ahead of him, he called out. "Mr. Carstairs?"

Whoever it was disappeared into a darkness which resolved itself into a thick hedge. Laughter sounded from beyond it, and Leon shivered again. Looking back toward the house, all he saw was a wall of fog. Even the torches were obscured. He took a tentative step forward and found himself in the entrance to a maze.

"Mr. Carstairs?"

"Come this way, mortal. We've been expecting you."

Leon turned toward the voice and saw a silver glow of light. He walked toward it, feeling claustrophobic on the narrow path between the hedge walls. Just when he thought he'd lost the way, another blob of torchlight would appear, leading him on. Finally, he reached an enclosed garden, at the center of which was a large wild rose bush, moonlight sparkling on the fog-damp foliage. On the other side of the shrub stood a figure in black.

"Mr. Carstairs?"

Somewhere in the night, a horn sounded. Not a car horn nor a party horn, but some primeval instrument that froze Leon's blood. The figure across the garden raised a horn to its lips and sounded an answering call. As it did so, the diadem across its brow flashed with starlight, forcing Leon to recall more of Patrick Carstairs' flight of fancy. Whoever this was, he perfectly matched the boy's description of Oberon, High King of Faerie.

King Oberon is tall and pale, clothed all in black but for his crown, which is made of stars.

Leon was furious. "Is this some sort of joke?" he spat at the figure. "You think you can make me change the boy's grade with this ridiculous fakery? By playing along with his fantasies? I came here to warn you that your son is a deviant, but now I see why. I shall inform the proper authorities first thing in the morning, Mr. Carstairs."

"You transgress, mortal. Tell me, what do you know of the Wild Hunt?"

Leon recalled Patrick's description of the Huntsman, a depraved thing no ten-year-old should have knowledge of.

Darker than night, but for his eyes, which shine red with lust for the blood the Wild Hunt demands.

Somewhere just beyond the hedge, a hound bayed. Others took up the call, a discordant symphony from hell.

"It isn't possible," Leon whispered. "The brat made you up out of Shakespeare and psychopathy. You're not real."

"We are an Elder Race. We existed long before your kind walked upright, and we will exist long after you have poisoned yourselves to death. I do not tolerate abuse of my subjects nor trespass upon our revels." The figure once again sounded its horn.

The answering call sounded almost simultaneously. Something massive broke through the hedge, slamming Leon to the ground and pinning him with heavy paws. Other howling beasts appeared, followed by pounding hooves as red-eyed horses, blacker than the night, leaped the hedge, led by one whose darkness engulfed the world.

"You're not real!" Leon Birch screamed as the Wild Hunt arrived for the kill.

ERIKA M SZABO
The Witch's One Stop Shop
ORGANS FOR SALE

The air was crisp and cool, signaling the arrival of autumn. The leaves had begun to turn to shades of fiery red and golden yellow, a beautiful backdrop for the second weekend of October in the early nineteen eighties. It was one of the last opportunities to sit around a campfire before winter's chill set in. Jack's father had recently built a firepit in the backyard, and a group of nine-year-old kids eagerly huddled around it, their faces lit up by the dancing flames. They roasted marshmallows on sticks and traded scary Halloween stories, trying to outdo each other with tales of ghosts and ghouls. Jack, a lanky boy with unruly jet-black hair, couldn't resist sharing his classic story about the ghost that haunted the spooky house in the woods.

However, Steve, his short blond friend, quickly protested, declaring that they had all heard it countless times before. "Come on, Jack! You told this story a gazillion times already."

But Jack persisted, determined to give them all goosebumps with his eerie storytelling skills. His face flushed with anger, and he was on the verge of snapping at Steve, but Claire, a tomboy who hated girly clothes and was known as the diplomat of their friend circle, stepped in. "Enough, you two!" she scolded the boys, shaking her head. "Steve, if you find Jack's story boring, why don't you tell a new story?"

"You tell a story, smarty-pants!" Steve retorted with a sneer. Despite his tendency to criticize others, he rarely had any original thoughts of his own to contribute. His sharp tongue was often used to deflect attention from his lack of creativity.

Claire's voice quivered as she spoke, "Okay. I'm going to tell you what I saw yesterday." She paused to take a deep breath before continuing, her eyes wide with fear of the memory. "Grandma and I went to the Witch's One Stop Shop, you know, in that spooky house that used to be empty. And Marie's mom, who works nearby, saw a ghost there when she was walking home late one night." The words hung in the air, thick with tension.

"Come on, Claire, you didn't see a ghost, did you?" Steve cackled.

Claire replied with a nervous tremor in her voice, "Of course not! It was in the middle of the afternoon. But I've seen something that scared the daylights out of me."

"What did you see?" Jack asked, his interest peaking.

"When we went into the store, there was a sign that said used organs for sale. And when the woman came out of the back door, I could swear she was a real witch. She wore black clothes, her hair in a messy bun, and she wore a black eyepatch over her right eye."

"That doesn't mean she's a witch!" Charlie looked at Claire wide-eyed.

"No?" Claire snapped. "She had bloody gloves on, and she just took them off and threw them in the garbage."

"Um…bloody gloves?" Jack shivered. "You mean…if, as you said, she's selling organs…"

"What?" Steve whispered. "Like kidneys and livers and hearts kinda organs? Naw, it can't be true!"

"I guess so…and what I saw made me think because I saw Marie's mom leaving the store with a small package in her hand that was smeared with blood," Claire said, wringing his fingers and taking a deep breath. "You guys know that Marie is very sick and waiting for the right organ donor who can give her a kidney, right?"

"Jack let out a heavy, sympathetic sigh. "Yes, poor Marie," he muttered.

"I went to visit her the other day," Claire continued. "Marie was asleep, but her mom insisted I wait for her to wake up. So, I sat in the living room and started reading the book I got for Marie. But I couldn't help overhearing Marie's parents talking in the kitchen. Her mom cried and said that there was still no match for Marie and asked Marie's dad what they were going to do. But then her father got angry and shouted that if they couldn't find a match soon, he'd have to buy a kidney on the black market. He said there are plenty of organs for sale; they just needed to find the right seller."

Steve let out a disbelieving laugh. "Come on, Claire. That's just...nobody would sell their own kidney, right?" But even as he said it, he felt a chill running down his spine.

"No, it's true!" Claire protested with conviction, her voice rising in pitch. She leaned forward, hands clenched into fists, determined to convince her friends. "I asked my dad when we got home, and he said it was true. He read in the papers that poor people in India are desperate and selling one of their kidneys to feed their families."

Charlie's eyes widened in horror as he whispered, "It must be true." His timid demeanor was replaced with fear and awe at the thought. "I heard my dad telling the UPS guy," stammered Charlie, his voice shaking, "that ruthless gangs kidnap kids and sell their organs to rich people."

"You don't think…" Jack stopped in mid-sentence, unable to finish his thought as fear consumed him. He had always been skeptical about stories, but now he couldn't deny the possibility. His mind raced with terrifying images of a powerful witch living in their quiet town.

The chatter of the group was suddenly interrupted by Martha, a lively girl with plump cheeks and red, curly hair. "I heard about her too!" she exclaimed, her eyes widening with intrigue. "My grandma says she's a strange woman. She lives all alone, and no one knows where she came from. She's got this creepy black cat and bought the old Smith house that everyone says is haunted." The group leaned in closer, eagerly listening to Martha's accounts of her grandmother's warnings. "Grandma said I must stay away from her because she's a witch, and she does black magic."

The mention of the black cat sent shivers down their spines as they imagined it prowling through the halls of the once-spooky house, now made even more sinister by its new owner. The children's chatter slowly subsided as the warm glow of the fire mesmerized them. They sat in a circle, lost in their own thoughts, the crackle of the flames and the distant hoots of owls filling the silence. As the full moon rose, casting long shadows, a chill crept into the air. The once cheerful atmosphere was now tinged with an eerie sense of mystery. With a quick goodbye and hurried steps, they made their way back home before darkness could fully envelop them in its embrace.

As the night wore on, Jack's mind became engulfed in a terrible nightmare. He tossed and turned; his body drenched in sweat as he fought against an unseen force. In his dream, he found himself tied to a cold, metal table by an old woman with wild hair and a black eye patch. His eyes widened in horror as he took in the sight of the room around him - it was filled with pale, lifeless bodies, their vacant eyes staring back at him. Jack's throat constricted as he tried to scream for help, but no sound escaped his lips. The old woman's bloodshot eye fixated on him, her toothless mouth opening in a cackling laugh that echoed through the bleak space. Jack, desperate to escape, felt trapped and helpless under the old woman's sinister gaze.

As the first rays of dawn crept through the window, Jack's eyes snapped open, and he sat up in bed, panting heavily and drenched in a cold sweat. The sound of his dad's loud snoring filled the house, along with the distant barking of a neighbor's dog. These familiar noises brought a sense of comfort to Jack as he tried to calm himself down. "I shouldn't have watched that horror movie with Steve. That's why I had that terrible dream," he muttered and reached for his phone and dialed his best friend's number. With the first ring, Steve picked up and answered in a hushed voice. "What? You okay?"

"I…I had the weirdest dream. You know, it was like the movie we watched, but the witch was in it too…and…" Jack replied in a trembling whisper.

"Me too," Steve admitted. "It was like...but it wasn't about the movie. Ugh! The witch had like livers and hearts in jars on the shelves in her shop and…I was scared out of my mind that she would cut my heart out and sell it."

The shared experience only added to the eerie feeling that hung in the air between them.

"It's good that it was only a dream. Let's try to go back to sleep," Steve said, and they hung up the phone.

Jack fell back into a restless slumber, his mind racing with tangled thoughts and half-formed dreams. When he heard the soft sounds of his parents moving about in the house, he stumbled downstairs to the cozy kitchen, still clad in his loose pajamas. As he made his way through the dimly lit hallway, he accidentally bumped into his dad, who was heading toward the backdoor. "Whoa there!" Jack's dad chuckled, reaching out to steady him. "You're up early. Is everything alright?" His face took on a look of concern as he noticed Jack's disheveled appearance. "You kids didn't stay outside as late as you usually do."

"Yeah, fine...we were just...it was cold," Jack replied, stepping aside to let his father open the door.

"Yes, it was a bit chilly." His dad turned and called out to his wife in a hurry, "I'm heading over to Tim's garage to pick up the parts I ordered. Do you want me to get something from town?"

"Oh, yes," Jack's mother smiled. "Olivia, you know, the woman who owns the Witch's One Stop Shop called that she has fresh liver today. I ordered some for dinner."

Jack's eyes grew wide with fear, his breath catching in his throat like a fish gasping for air. His mind raced with horrifying possibilities. *Does the witch really sell liver? Is she butchering people in her basement?* He shuddered at the thought of what kind of sinister dealings were happening just beyond the walls of her store.

His mother noticed his distress and asked, her voice filled with worry, "What's wrong, Jack? You look as pale as a ghost." She reached out to touch his forehead.

"I-I'm fine, Mom," Jack stammered, pushing her hand away. But he knew he was far from fine. The images of severed limbs and bloody organs haunted his mind, causing him to break out in a cold sweat.

***

As the sun reached its peak, casting short shadows, the kids gathered in Jack's darkened room. The air was thick with tension.

"It must be just gossip or a misunderstanding," Martha probed, her voice laced with skepticism.

Steve shook his head vehemently. "Did you not hear what Claire and Jack said yesterday? This is serious."

"We can't just believe everything we hear," Martha insisted, her tone becoming firmer. "We have to find out what's really going on over there." The urgency in her voice hung heavy in the stillness of the room.

They decided to take a ride to the witch's shop.

***

As they approached the house, they hid their bikes in a nearby ditch and crept cautiously toward the building. Ducking behind a gnarled bush, they peeked, watching the weathered building. Above the door hung a sign: "The Witch's One Stop Shop".

Steve's heart quickened at the sight, and he couldn't help but imagine the horrors that must take place within those doors. "That must be where she butchers the bodies and sells the body parts," he whispered, his voice trembling with fear.

138

Their eyes remained fixed on the closed door, expecting to see something horrific emerge with each passing second. They stood frozen in terror as a middle-aged woman stepped out, her black dress and disheveled dark hair giving her a menacing appearance. A black eyepatch covered her right eye, adding to the sinister aura that surrounded her.

"Let's get out of here before she sells our livers too!" Jack's voice trembled with fear as he scrambled up from his spot on the ground and raced to his bike. The others quickly followed suit, their hearts pounding in their chests. Claire could feel a scream building up inside her, threatening to burst forth at any moment.

"From now on, I'm a vegetarian. I swear!" Jack huffed as he pedaled away in a great hurry, followed by his friends.

The woman halted in her tracks and turned to face the commotion on the other side of the street. Her eyes scanned the group of children frantically paddling away. "I wonder what could have frightened them," she mused aloud, turning to the stocky man who had just emerged from the store carrying a small table.

He shrugged his gaze fixed on the children. "Your guess is as good as mine," he replied. "I'm going to take this table, and can I have that goose with a black feather in its tail?" He gestured toward the flock of geese in the fenced-in yard next to the store with a hopeful tone in his voice.

"Sure," she replied. "The table is sixteen dollars. When will you pick up the goose?"

"The day before Halloween," the man said, handing her the money. "We'll have a houseful of guests, and my wife wants to cook the goose the day before. By the way, how's your eye?" The man asked with genuine concern. "It must be hard to take care of the shop and to look after the birds when your eye is covered. Let me know if you need any help."

The woman shrugged and smiled. "Thank you for offering, but I'll be fine, don't worry." She turned to face him. The doctor took out the glass fragment, and he said it wouldn't affect my vision after it healed." A proud smile spread across her face. "Besides, I've been raising chickens, ducks, and geese for a long time. I can feed them with both eyes closed."

***

As Jack pushed away his dinner plate, refusing to touch the food that sat in front of him, a look of discomfort crossed his face.

"What's wrong, Jack?" his mother asked with great concern. "It's fried goose liver, your favorite!"

"Goose liver? But we thought…" Jack stammered and sighed, and then a bright smile lit up on his face. He confessed why he couldn't bring himself to take a bite. "She…she's not a real witch then?" he asked.

With a chuckle trying to escape his lips, his father patiently explained, "Of course not, son! Her name is Olivia. She moved here from another state where she had an antique store and kept the name for her new shop. And she raises and sells poultry. That's where I got the goose liver from."

"But she has that sign 'Organs for Sale,' so we thought…because people have organs in their bodies," Jack said.

"Oh, you silly boy!" Jack's mother laughed. "The music school bought new musical instruments, and Olivia sells the used organs in her shop."

Jack let out a sigh of relief, feeling foolish for his misunderstanding, and dug into his dinner. He finished quickly and eagerly ran up to his room to call his friends.

His father shook his head in amusement. "Kids and their wild imagination," he said with a smile.

MARTHA PEREZ
FALLEN ANGEL

Isabella

My dark wings sent me on the wrong path; losing faith in Heaven made me a fallen angel with black, broken wings and a halo smashed to smithereens. What used to be bright lights, harps, and happiness now has me sitting in darkness with screaming spirits wailing. I stay with monsters, beasts, zombies, wolves, hellhounds, and Satan. My heart breaks and bleeds every minute of the day. There is no rest, just chaos. I am on bent knees, weeping for God to forgive me, but there is no answer as I pray for forgiveness. I'm afraid for my soul, the unknown black hole of Hell, being alone with my scary thoughts, and my pathic discretions with splintering nightmares. It's my only plea to save myself. I can't eat or sleep; there's a deep voice. "My fallen angel, all mine," Satan rambles. He laughs, taunting every night, tears of misery falling to the ground. He surrounds my legs with snakes. My screams are raucous; all critters surround me like a feast with no getaway; I'm near a crevasse pit.

It's my fault for losing my faith and grace; there's no going back. A wrong crossroad to a path of wickedness. Satan was charming at first, changing his face so you don't know who he is, reeling me in, saying, "Come with me to Wonderland," Standing before me was a handsome figure who was evil with no wings, spreading evilness in the dark woods. I could never trust his words again, grinning like a black cat that swallowed the canary. He weakens my knees like no other; Satan is evil who looks for weakness. Shackles bind me down, my ankles are sore, and a bleeding neck with a leather choker confines me, choking my airway. A fire surrounds me with no escape; the flames are high, and it's so hot and unbearable that sweat drips from my forehead. I'm not too fond of it here.

I've suffered enough. I can't take the heat; Satan's voice screams, and he laughs, mocking me. It isn't amicable, it's cruel. The creepy crawlies are eating me alive. I'm getting weaker, my mouth requires drinking water, and black beetles are lagging on my body. My screams are louder to free me; all I ever wanted was to be in Heaven. One mistake brings me heartache. All I get is burning Hell, which he comes to me with a teasing grin; he's a fire of brimstone. I'm scared. The demons torture the souls, screeching in pain; the beast's nails are black, and they have sharp teeth, faces, and bodies with scarred marks and no wings in sight. They keep screaming, making me crazy.

"I will kill you over and over again, Isabella. No one disobeys me, and you will never see the light of day, my sweet dear; you have fallen into the pit of Hell. Temptation is tempting, making a deal with Satan; there is no going back; you're mine, all mine to have. Treasure forever; you're such a beauty with broken black wings. You will beg me to stop hurting you every minute of every day. The beast wants your flesh; he always loves the taste of an angel. Come to me, Isabella, and show me who's king. Reveal the ground I walk on. I'm your master for eternity; don't you forget it and stop crying, my dear?" Satan speaks.

The wolves are howling and hungry; they want to eat me. I must have the strength to endure, or they will bite my flesh, paying for my sins. The demons get the blade and cut my arm and leg, then the other with knives and arms, gore spilling down my body; cries are known this is maltreatment. This will be my curse for imperishability for making wrong choices, so many regrets in my darkness of wickedness, and a hell of no hope or faith. My lips chapped with cuts, and skin-and-bones dark shadows appeared out of nowhere. This is madness. I'm lying on the filthy ground; roaches make me open my eyes. I look up with tears, a full moon and luminous effervescent, *"Angel, will soon be home?"* My tears continued to descend. Oh, God is talking to me. The pain didn't go away, though; there was nothing to gain in this inferno. I want to leave this place of evilness. Burning pit demons rage Satan worship; fallen angels are here forever.

Days go by like a burst of gushing speed and squalling storm screams overwhelming the mind. The heat makes me ill. The fallen angels are getting tortured. The sinner's fate is death, pure destruction, and watching the horrible scene destroy and punish the soul.

The following night, I woke with no shackles or chokers on my neck and relaxed my airway. I got up from the ground and ran, not looking back, but I heard the hellhound following me, wishing to have my white wings and fly away like a bird. Is this the end, or is it a wicked game Satan is playing? The forest is dark and scary, and hiding is my best option, so *I* made a small hut of branches and leaves and started to think. *How I became an angel when I was a human on earth, my boyfriend murdered me. He had this awful rage that couldn't help himself, so one night, I told him I was leaving, had enough, and he pushed me and stabbed me until my last breath. I went up the loveliest steps and followed the light. Heaven awaits pure happiness and no pain serving God; my beautiful halo shined like the stars. I earned my white wings, saving a teenager from jumping off a bridge. I mistakenly guided a sinner to Heaven when he was supposed to go downstairs to Hell. I didn't follow the rules: you can't save everyone; my wings were stripped and replaced with black wings, and I became a fallen angel.* I was now stuck in Hell with Satan and his monsters. They are hunting me down safely for the moment. I take a deep breath and another and close my eyes; the silence comforts me, and I fall into a deep slumber until I hear some cracking. I swallow with fear as they find me. I don't want to go back, but then I hear a voice come out. Isabella he knew my name, and I run the opposite way, stumbling on the ground. Crows surround me, it starts to storm, pouring rain, and the mud makes walking challenging. It's like quicksand; it is quicksand sinking with no escape. Maybe now my soul will be in peace going down under six feet deep when I see the light, a hand lifting me from the deep mud, carrying me to a lovely waterfall, and washing the quicksand off my body. My long, silky black hair was braided and now loose. The stranger removes my hair from my face; he's an angel. He covers me with his white wings to dry my body, keeping me safe for a while; then Satan takes us by surprise and throws me into one of his caves. He's torturing the angel that was saving me. I pray to God to save the angel, but there is no answer; feeling guilty, tears decent for his soul.

I skulk from my dark room, and it's a hideaway that Satan keeps us in. I want to be free, spreading my black wings; Hell is deviant, and I become a confused and saddened fallen angel. I don't know how to survive with wild demons, evil beasts, and creatures of the night crawling on my feet, nipping and biting my feet again. Satan is a killer, a warped, rebelled angel. He's as dark as they come, God, who allows him power in a fallen world and hosts demons. I can't tolerate him much more. I have no definition of what comes or what goes. The crows are waiting for me to die. No one taught me to be brave, and my thoughts are everywhere.

My heart shattered, missing Heaven. I wish this was a dream; my soul is going through a poorly lit journey. Nothing has changed; it's so hot, drawing me in an awful way as the minutes tick-tock. I've been in a place called Hell. Pieces of bones break in my body. I can't mend the mistakes. So much has happened since Heaven, and I am losing faith. My life is different. I have to learn to accept everything is dim.

I saw the light of day. My nights are with prayers, but the dark soul brings me into terror. I know it's my destiny. I stare in the darkness at a bed of black roses. I keep thinking of what could have been. Its fragrance is dead; black roses don't bring peace or hope to me. The fire pit flaming, the black crows circle me, and dark souls scream for mercy again; it's a never-ending story.

No lights, only darkness. All I want is freedom. My dreams are real, dark, and raw. I can't just let go of a good soul. My heart aches for the angel from Heaven now; he walks in evil and Hell. My heart is filled with pain and sorrow.

I'm a fallen angel locked and bound, shedding tears with nothing to do or say.

After the tears fall, I'm still a fallen angel, and I can't step toward the light. I have made so many downfalls.

There are choices we make that have terrible consequences. I didn't believe in salvation until now. I lift my arms with gushing tears. The light doesn't shine, and my wings don't fly; the scent of wildflowers invades my nostrils. My home is Hell. Time is running out for me. Will I make it the following day?

"My Isabella, you have suffered enough. I have unlocked the doors and saved your soul and the angel who tried to save you. I will lift you and take both back to Heaven." God has spoken.

I see rainbows and no creatures, angels singing, no more screaming following the rules of the Goddess skies of the promised land, no more crossroads to Hell.

Satan

God may have won this time, but soon, another fallen angel will fall from up above, and I will catch them, and then the darkness will rise, and games will begin. I am in a rage, so I walk to the sinners hanging like a piece of meat. I slice and dice, and mice fear me, and away they disappear; it's nice being me. The man begs for mercy, but I don't have any; all I give is pain; it gives me a high. The feeling is so good, closing my red eyes and relishing the sensation. Beware of me; it's Halloween; the bats and crows with other monsters are by my side.

***

"I found my light and left my black wings behind. Embracing my white wings, I fly with grace and power to the highest tower. A shining halo above my head follows the steps of paradise to receive happiness. Pray for your salvation with each step of healing. And believing in your faith will help you become a protector and a guardian angel," Martha Perez.

THE
PUMPKIN'S
CURSE
MARTHA
PEREZ

I have always felt an odd trepidation towards pumpkins since my early years. Their twisted faces made me feel as if they were watching. This fear stuck with me into my teens. Mom, a teacher, is always busy grading papers late into the night. Despite her busy schedule, I still felt safe until we had to move, leaving behind my friends and family.

Mom bought a house in a small town called Dark Creek, where she got a job at a school just a few blocks away. Our new address is 1300 Dead End Street. The house is ancient, with broken windows and glass scattered everywhere. The backyard borders the forest. And, of course, there's a basement. No doubt, it holds stories of its own.

Mom and I are waiting for the movers to bring our furniture, and a few men from town offered to fix the windows. I found it strange how they whispered among themselves as if keeping some big secret. But I ignored them, focusing instead on helping Mom clean and unpack.

We ordered pizza and shared it with the workers. By the time they were getting ready to leave, it was already dark. They promised to return the next day.

That night, lying in bed, I hear noises from the basement. The sound is eerie, sending chills down my spine. I don't want to go down there. But, like the people in horror movies, I feel compelled to go where I shouldn't.

Instead of running away, I head toward the basement door. My heart pounds, and the flashlight I'm holding flickers on and off, just like a scene from a typical horror story.

I open the door, and it creaks like old houses do. The basement light doesn't work. With each step, a strange ticking sound grows louder. Suddenly, I bump into someone, and we both scream.

"What are you doing down here, Scarlett?" Mom says, her voice shaky.

"Mom! You scared me half to death!" I snap, catching my breath. "I thought I heard something down here."

"I'm sorry, sweetheart," she says, rubbing her arms. "I found some boxes left by the previous owners. Look at this." She pulls out a pumpkin with a terrifying grin. "Doesn't this look like the Joker from Batman? I bet they loved Halloween."

"Ugh, I hate Halloween. And I really hate pumpkins," I tell her, shuddering.

We head back upstairs, and the next day, I see the same pumpkin on the porch. The workers laugh about it, comparing it to the Joker's signature smile. But to me, it looks sinister. I throw it in the trash and try to shake off the creepy feeling as I continue unpacking.

Later, I decide to take a ride to the store for some snacks and magazines. As I'm locking up my bike, a guy about my age stares at me.

"Hey there," he says. "Never seen you around here. You new in town?"

"Yeah, we just moved to 1300 Dead End Street," I reply.

The guy's expression changes. "That old house? Your family must be brave to stay there."

I frown. "Are you trying to scare me?"

"My name's Donald Winters," he says, shaking his head. "I'm not trying to scare you, but that place has a reputation. I could tell you more if you want. Maybe we could meet tomorrow at the river."

"Nice to meet you, Donald. I'm Scarlett," I respond. "I'm definitely interested in hearing more."

As I ride home, I can't shake the feeling that there's something Donald knows about our house that I don't. When I pull up to the porch, I freeze. The pumpkin I had thrown away earlier… is back.

"What the heck?" I mutter, rushing inside. "Mom! Are you home?"

I peek out the window, but Mom's car isn't in the driveway. She's probably still at work. Maybe one of the workers thought it would be funny to put the pumpkin back as a prank. But I'm not laughing. Feeling uneasy, I bag it up and throw it in the trash again.

Later, when Mom gets home, we start cooking dinner together.

"I'm glad you decided to put that pumpkin back on the porch," she says casually.

"What? I threw the pumpkin away, Mom!" I exclaim.

I run to the porch, only to see the pumpkin sitting right where it had been. This is getting weird. Someone must be messing with my mind. Frustrated, I grab a market bag, toss the pumpkin inside, and dump it in the neighbor's trash bin.

We eat dinner, and after reading for a while, I check on Mom. She has already fallen asleep, so I gently cover her with a blanket.

At least the men finished fixing the house without pulling any more pranks. But I can't shake the nagging thought that the pumpkin will reappear again. It's becoming a mystery I can't ignore.

The next morning, we hear voices outside. The police are at Teddy Shaw's house. Had something happened? Mom and I go to see what's going on. Detective Jerry Marsh asks if we heard anything unusual last night. We tell him no.

"Teddy's body is missing," the detective says gravely. "All that was left behind was his head... and an axe."

They take the head and axe as evidence. The townspeople whisper among themselves, sharing rumors. When Mom and I go to the diner for breakfast, everyone stares at us like we're hiding something.

Afterward, Mom heads to school, while I go to meet Donald at the river creek before class. He's leaning against an oak tree when I arrive.

"Hey, I heard what happened next door," Donald says, his face grim. "Teddy was a good man, and now his body's gone. If I were you, I'd take your mom and leave as fast as you can. Save yourselves before it's too late… like it was for my family."

I frown, trying to process his words. "I did some research online," I tell him. "A guy named Ozzy Stone disappeared from our house, and the pumpkin looks just like him. Could he be the one killing people?"

Donald's face hardens. "He murdered my entire family. The townspeople came after him with knives, stabbed him until his last breath, and buried him in the woods. But he comes back every Halloween."

Tomorrow is Halloween. Panic surges through me. I rush home, desperate to find Mom, but she is nowhere to be found. I try calling her cell, but there is no answer.

I head to the school, where the teenagers are holding a Halloween dance in the auditorium. The music is loud, and everyone is wearing masks. My heart stops when I spot it—a Joker pumpkin head. But this time, it has a body.

I stare, recognizing the body. It's Teddy's. He's dancing to "Stayin' Alive" by the Bee Gees.

Suddenly, he sees me.

Before I can react, he rushes toward me.

Donald appears out of nowhere, bumping into me. "Run!" he shouts, grabbing my arm.

We bolt out of the school, the Joker pumpkin chasing us. The teens inside continue dancing, oblivious to the nightmare happening just outside. Donald and I finally make it to my house, where we wait anxiously for Mom.

By morning, she still hasn't returned. The sun rises briefly before the sky turns gray. Lightning flashes, and the wind howls, shaking the trees so violently that some rip free from the ground. The whole scene is spine-chilling.

Halloween has arrived, and it brings something sinister with it. Black crows perch in the trees, cawing in eerie unison.

I wake Donald. "Look outside," I say, voice trembling.

He glances through the window and pales. "They're coming," he mutters, his voice filled with dread.

"Who's coming?!" I ask, terrified and confused.

"Have you checked the basement?" he asks suddenly.

"No… I'll grab the flashlight," I say.

I find the flashlight in the kitchen drawer, along with a knife for protection. With the basement light still broken, each step down feels like a leap into darkness. My heart pounds as I hear a soft moaning.

I skip the last few steps and rush toward the sound.

"Mom?!" I cry, horrified to find her tied to a chair. I quickly cut the ropes with the knife.

"Who did this to you?" I ask, my voice shaking.

"Scarlett," she gasps, "my mind was playing tricks on me. A man with a Joker pumpkin face... he tied me up and rocked me back and forth like a lunatic. I begged him to leave me alone, and then he just got up and left."

"You're safe now, Mom," I reassure her, hugging her tightly.

We help her upstairs, but when I glance outside, thousands of black crows are in the trees, watching. Donald told me that black crows are a bad omen, symbols of death. Is he in a trance?

I hurry to close all the curtains, but when I peek outside, the Joker pumpkin stands in the yard, waiting.

I open the door cautiously. He stares at me with cold, dead eyes.

"Oh, my dear Scarlett," he says in a low, raspy voice. "Your mind isn't playing tricks on you. Every year on Halloween, the family living in this house must die."

I slam the door shut. How dare he threaten to take our lives. It's Halloween night.

My fears crawl back, my hands trembling. Every year, he finds a way to murder the people who move into this cursed place.

I feel a creeping sensation like spiders swarming over my body and the walls. Panicked, I glance around, but nothing's there. I collapse to my knees, hands on my face, tears flowing. It sounds ridiculous, but I can't shake the feeling.

It's still dark. Outside, kids are knocking on doors for candy, unaware of the danger. "Go away!" I scream. "The evil will kill you! Run while you still can!"

The Joker pumpkin man grins from ear to ear, his twisted smile scaring the children away. He's messing with my mind, feeding on my fear. I feel it deep in my gut. He's trying to break me, to make me weak, so he can take me and Mom.

Tears run down my face as I sit on the living room floor, paralyzed with terror. This place never felt like home. It's too dark, too strange. Even if I wanted to move, my body won't let me. I try to keep my focus, but my thoughts keep returning to the basement, where we found the Joker pumpkin head. The only place where terror seems to roam free. That cold room drives me to the brink of madness.

Then it happens.

Mom appears, holding an axe, her eyes vacant. She's trying to kill me.

"You must die, Scarlett," she mutters, her voice eerily flat.

I run to the basement, where the Joker pumpkin is waiting for me. He grabs me, his grip cold and unyielding. I see Mom, still holding the axe, advancing toward me.

He got to her.

He's controlling her.

Everything goes black.

One year later...

A new family moves into 1300 Dead End Street. They have a son and a daughter. As they settle in, the son finds two strange pumpkin heads in the basement and decides to place them on the front porch.

The mailman arrives, and as he delivers their mail, he takes a long, hard look at the pumpkins.

"They look familiar," he says, frowning. "Two people went missing from this house last year."

The daughter comes out, holding a photograph. "This is Scarlett," she says, showing him the picture. "Doesn't she look just like one of the pumpkins?"

The family grows uneasy. They decide to call the realtor for an explanation about the previous owners.

A short while later, a man knocks on the door. "Hi, my name is Donald Winters," he introduces himself. "What seems to be the matter?"

The mother, concern etched on her face, asks, "What happened to the people who used to live here?"

Donald's expression remains calm. "They left without a word. Old news in this town. Enjoy your new home. If I don't see you next month..." He grins, "...Happy Halloween."

With that, Donald walks away, leaving the family staring at the pumpkins on their porch, unsure whether to believe the story or fear it.

Pumpkin Patch

Strong winds sweep through the pumpkin heads, transforming the night into a sprawling, haunted pumpkin patch. Panic fills the air, and the Joker pumpkin watches with a twisted smile, knowing that the inevitable is always predictable. We are drawn into a darkness beyond our control.

Halloween begins with treats, children in masks, and fun. But after bedtime, the real horrors emerge. People vanish without a trace. The cemetery is disturbed, its headstones slanting, as crows circle the dead and torment the living. Ghosts stalk the night, their presence turning deadly.

Run, if you can. Otherwise, you'll become part of the cursed pumpkin patch.

Perhaps someone can escape this nightmare, freed from the grip of evil. But as the rain pours down in torrents, washing away all hope, one thing becomes clear...

There is nowhere to run.

Nowhere to hide.

It's impossible to survive the night.

- Martha Perez

MASTER BRAHM'S STUDIO
SHEBAT LEGION

The students, carefully selected from multiple kingdoms, fiefs, and villages, stood dutifully at their stations, clutching paintbrushes. Their eyes focused on the empty canvas on an easel before them; they waited for the master to speak.

"What do you see before you?" The master, a wizened man of advanced years, asked, "What do you see?"

An overly eager lad from the isle of Winsey raised his free hand, and the master raised an eyebrow and motioned for him to speak.

"A blank space, waiting,"

The master grunted, then sneered, "Poetic, but incorrect." He looked around at the silent group and grunted again. "Waiting, yes, but what you see, ahh..." His voice trailed off, and his eyes narrowed. "What you see before you cannot be put into simple words; it is what you feel, what comes from within if you listen. It is what you allow if you permit yourself."

The master glared at the wilting student from Winsey, "Not all of you will do that; not all of you are capable." He whirled, turning his back on the nervous student, and the boy visibly sagged in relief.

Master Brahm hummed to himself as he chose a paintbrush from the collection on his desk. There were many, all different sizes, ranging from a large flat brush to the most delicate of all, a brush that sported only one long hair. His choice was made, and the master asked, "What is this?" He held a medium-sized brush in front of him like a sword.

Not a single student dared raise a hand.

"What? Not a one?" the master scoffed. "No one brave enough to venture a guess? I will give you a clue," he chuckled. "What is a tool when it isn't a tool?"

The room remained silent, but one girl fidgeted, and the master's eyes were on her like a hawk. "You girl, you have a thought? A musing? A slight glimmer of understanding?"

The girl, a waif found in a small village from beyond the Blue Mountains, straightened her shoulders and fixed her pale, blue eyes on the master.

"What I should say, I will not, for I think we are here to learn what it is you want us to learn," she said, then boldly added, "I think whatever I would say, you would find fault."

The master stared, then guffawed, slapping his knee with one hand, the other still clutching his paintbrush.

"Quite right, quite right. You are an egg, barely pecking at your shell; you know nothing, struggling to free yourself," he laughed. "Peck, peck, peck! But" he rasped," Miss Thisbe from nowhere, you will share with me your thoughts, or you shall leave my studio!" He thrust the paintbrush into her face. "What is this?"

Thisbe didn't flinch, and most of the room looked at her with admiration as she answered, "Sacrifice."

"So," Master Brahm whispered.

The master stared into Thisbe's eyes, and she stared back without fear. Master Brahm held her gaze a moment, then turned to face the rest of the class.

"I could just tell you, yes? I am the teacher, yes?"

There was a great nodding of heads and whispers of consent, and the master shouted, "It is, yes, 'Master Brahm! No Master Brahm.' Do they not teach you manners from wherever you were found?"

The students mutedly replied, "Yes, Master Brahm."

"That is fine if one were a mouse, which I am not, speak so a man can hear you!"

"Yes, Master Brahm," the class said in unison in a louder voice.

The master used his brush again, painting the air before him as he spoke. "What is this? A tool? Yes, this is a tool, but more than that, you are a tool for that tool; it is part of you, as much as your eyes or your heart. It is an extension of whatever makes you, you." The master pointed here and there with the brush. "I do not expect eggs like yourselves to understand." He looked at Thisbe." Most of you. But you must. You must!"

The master glared around the room. "For if you do not and cannot, you do not belong in this room."

The sound of a distant bell came, and the master threw the brush across the room over the trembling students' heads. "Dismissed."

"Overly zealous," whispered the other masters.

"Bully," whimpered most of the students.

After a brief lunch, class resumed, and the master plonked a vase down with such venom that water spilled over its side. Contained in the vessel were an assortment of wilted flowers.

"What do you see?" The master pointed at a boy who sat at the front of the class and gulped in relief as the question seemed rhetorical. "And you?" the master pointed, "You there, and what about you?" The master gestured across the room.

The master lectured, "All will see something different. Look!" He whirled, almost knocking over the vase in his zeal. "You will see the daisy first, and you," he pointed again, "you will see the rose first, but all," he waved his arms, "are a collection and seen together, so which is the subject? Is it the first thing you see? Is it all of them together?"

The class remained silent.

"Is it a sow? Is it some automobile?" Master Brahm giggled at his joke and added, "We shall see what it is you see. You will take a stick of charcoal, and you will have no more than three minutes to show me."

The students scrambled, etching quickly upon the pads of paper set at their station while Master Brahm turned over an hourglass that trickled the minutes that passed. After which, he turned the flower arrangement a touch to the left, flipped the hourglass, and roared, "Again!" And then, another three minutes, and another.

After an hour passed, the master gestured his students to stop, and they wearily put down what remained of their charcoal, holding their breath as the old man shuffled among them, looking here and there, sometimes stopping and muttering to himself, other times passing a student's work without so much as a glance.

"So," asked Master Brahm. "What have we learned?"

There was silence.

"Miss Thisbe, from nowhere, what have you learned?"

"The eyes are traitors," Thisbe answered calmly.

Master Brahm roared with as much exasperation as delight, "Yes, they are indeed!"

And so began a relationship between the two that could not be said to be based upon respect exactly but of a mutual antagonism based on something like it, the master attacking Thisbe with questions and her responding calmly and precisely, but far worse, correctly, often enraging Master Brahm.

The rest of the term carried along in much the same fashion. Some students improved under the zealous eye of Master Brahm, while others miserably failed to do so, leaving the class to take up other pursuits such as pottery or sculpting and never to touch a paintbrush again.

It should be said that while Master Brahm's methods were often terrifying, his knowledge was great, and he did his best to impart it, regardless of the process. His methods raised eyebrows among his peers, but his reputation as a great artist and teacher preceded him, and after all, he was an old man, his health clearly deteriorating.

"Observe." Master Brahm pointed at the bird who sat on a perch in a cage on a stool. "Our feathered friend is mortal and, like all things mortal, will die soon enough. You, as artists, whether with color, black and white, or whatever medium, give immortality where none existed. It is a great responsibility."

"Yes, Master Brahm," chanted the students.

"It could be said that you take the essence of this life and then transform it!"

"Yes, Master Brahm."

The master gave way to a coughing fit and staggered back to his desk. Thisbe watched, her blue eyes calm, a slight smile on her otherwise expressionless face.

As the end of the term approached, the students were informed they would have to present a minimum of five paintings or drawings approved by the master in order to pass. At this point, less than half the original class remained.

On the fateful day, Brahm shuffled to stand before each student's offerings, catching his breath and stopping when he reached the paintings Thisbe had produced.

On canvas were the likenesses of each student who had quit the class to pursue other pursuits.

The master looked at each painting, then began again at the first, mumbling to himself, "Yes, quite the likeness, yes, yes."

In truth, the likeness of the departed students was more than remarkable; they seemed to have a life to them that leaped off the canvas.

"Well," wheezed Master Brahm to the stoic Miss Thisbe. "Well, well, well. And do you still believe that your paintbrush is a sacrifice? A job well done, and you have clearly paid attention."

"Yes," said Thisbe, reaching for a painting that had thus remained uncovered. The paintbrush is a tool of sacrifice. And yes, I have paid close attention." With dignity, she removed the covering to reveal a painting of Master Brahm.

The other students gasped.

Master Brahm emerged from the painting, displaying more life than the man who stood before it.

"I should add, "said Thisbe, "a sacrifice made by the subject, not the artist."

"What?" Master Brahm gasped, then fell, clutching his chest, "You, you can't…"

"But I can," answered Thisbe. She knelt by the fallen master's side, placing his head in her lap as his lips turned blue. His eyes sought hers as she whispered, "Thank you, master, you have taught me well."

Robert Allen Lupton
BROOMSTICKS &
CHOCOLATE

Agatha couldn't help herself, so she swept the porch with her broom before she used the oversized door knocker. It was a bad reproduction of the head of Bela Lugosi's Dracula holding a single link of a heavy chain in his fanged mouth.

A short octogenarian woman who could have been Margaret Hamilton's double answered the door. "About time, Cousin Agatha. It's almost sunset, and the trick-or-treaters will be starting."

"Don't bristle at me. This is a new broom, and I just whisked in from Cincinnati. This isn't your first Halloween; I suspect you've got a handle on things."

"I do. Come inside, and let's get ready for the children."

Agatha leaned her broom against the wall inside the door. "This is a Boeing Stratoduster, right off the assembly line. Free to me because I'm a beta tester. Thought I'd try it for a spell."

Endora inspected the broomstick. "Boeing? It's a miracle you didn't crash on takeoff."

"Jealous much? You're still flying that old Curtis Twin Stick, aren't you?"

"It's a classic and the most stable broomstick ever manufactured. It belonged to my grandmother. She flew 36 missions during World War Two."

"She's my grandmother, too. That's such a bewitching tale, but my mom said that Grandma spent the war working in a defense plant in upstate New York putting protection spells on aircraft."

"She was a witch just like us. She told me that the defense plant was just a cover story. The Curtis was the fastest broom on the planet. She'd finish her shift at the Curtis-Wright plant, sweep across the Atlantic, make a bomber escort run, bewitch a V-2, and then shuffle back to Buffalo in time to clock in."

Agatha petted a large black cat, Ashtoreth, Endora's familiar. "Ashtoreth looks healthy and happy, cousin, but I came for Halloween, not a history lesson. Are we ready for the children?"

"I was born ready. Ashtoreth loves Halloween. We'll take turns with the kids. I'll go first and you take the second group. The children love my house because I don't do Halloween like everyone else."

"How does that work? Don't the children get upset?"

"Not at all. When I answer the door, they don't say trick-or-treat. I do. They always say trick, and then I do a trick for them. Different tricks for different kids. I sometimes make their flashlights talk or their costumed wings real. I make the jack-o'-lanterns or my Bela Lugosi door knocker talk."

"That's real magic, Endora. No one can know that magic is real."

"Relax, Cousin. The only magic I do for the children are parlor tricks, and they wear off like fairy gold when they leave my yard. Most of the parents who live around here visited my house when they were young, and the rest wouldn't believe it anyway. I'm just a harmless old lady. It's fun, and it makes Halloween a little more special for the children."

"Clang, clang, clang went Bela Lugosi. Endora opened the door and said, "Trick or treat."

Three princesses shouted, "Trick."

Ashtoreth slipped out the door, brushed against the girls' legs, and then slunk back into the house. Endora thought for a moment and then touched the girl's tiaras one at a time. The plastic headpieces glowed brighter than sparklers on the Fourth of July.

The princesses laughed and danced. Ashtoreth danced with them. Like real sparklers, the tiaras soon went out, and the three girls walked quickly to their mothers waiting on the sidewalk. One woman cupped her hands and yelled, "Thanks, Endora. You've still got it, girl."

Two boys ran onto the front porch. Endora smiled at them. "Wow, I love your costumes. Who are you supposed to be?"

"I'm Speed Racer, and Greg is Astro Boy. Manga comic characters. Japanese."

"Can't say as I've ever been to Japan. Trick or treat, boys.? Trick or treat?"

"Trick."

"Agatha, help me with this one. These boys want a trick."

Agatha waved her little finger, and Speed Racer's helmet lit up like a futuristic computer screen. Data flashed inside the faceplate, visible only to the wearer, and scrolled rapidly in several colors, using several languages, known and unknown. The young man was mesmerized.

Astro Boy lifted a few inches off the porch and floated in the air. He spun around twice and then landed. His eyes were bright with happiness. "Thank you, that was so cool. May we have another trick?"

"One trick per customer. Off with you now. Others are waiting."

"May we get back in line?"

Endora shook her finger. "Don't be a greedy gut. Come back next year unless you're too old."

Astro Boy frowned. "How will I know if I'm too old?"

"You'll know, but here's some hints. If you're taller than me, you're too old. If you have a driving license, you're too old. I used to say that if you can read cursive, you're too old, but no one learns to read cursive anymore."

Astro Boy looked confused. "I've never read anything written by Cursive. Did he write fantasy stories?"

"Not to be graphic, but that proves my point," said Endora. "Off with you now. Others are waiting."

***

Two short frontiersmen hurried toward the house. Endora recognized them as the Boone twins, named Daniel and Squire by parents with either a sense of humor or an overdeveloped sense of history. She closed the door so the boys could knock on it. Daniel tapped Bella Lugosi's face with his Red Ryder BB Gun.

Endora opened the door. "Don't shoot, Daniel. Trick or treat?"

"Can't shoot nothing, Miss Endora. Mom wouldn't let me bring no BBs. Squire and me don't want no trick or a treat. We want help. We was robbed."

"Daniel, I'm not the grammar police, but I think you mean to say, 'We were robbed.'"

164

"Yes, we was. Me and Squire trick'r treated by ourselves for the first time tonight. Dad's at work, and Mom's passing out candy at our house. We been to more than a hundred houses. Now all of our candy's gone."

"That's terrible. Here, take a couple of popcorn balls and tell Auntie Endora what happened."

Daniel stuffed a big bite of popcorn ball into his mouth, and while he chewed, Squire answered. "It was terrible. We were on Elm Street, and the Kruger brothers, Mike and Freddy, came out of nowhere. Mike had on a stupid Captain Kirk mask. They're big. Both are in High School. They pushed me down and grabbed my sack. Mike held Danny's arms and Freddy took his candy too. They laughed at us and ran away."

Daniel swallowed, but he still sprayed popcorn when he talked. "They're gonna keep stealing candy all night."

Agatha smiled. "If they eat all that candy, their teeth will rot out."

Squire grumbled, "We were hoping you'd help us a lot sooner than that."

Endora brushed sticky popcorn off her dress. Ashtoreth licked the stray kernels off the porch before they stopped moving. "Of course, we'll help. Candy thieves deserve no mercy. Do you know which way they went?"

Squire rubbed his face and smeared his burnt cork beard. "Yeah, they got in Freddy's car. It's a Frankenstein car that they patched together from the junkyard. Yellow door from one car, black door from another, and the hood is baby poop green. The rest of the body is white streaked with rust."

Agatha interrupted. "I saw that car when I flew in. I couldn't imagine it could run."

Daniel licked most of the corn syrup off his fingers and then wiped them on his pants. "We don't have no cell phones, or we'd have called the police. Please call them for us."

"I think we'll leave the authorities out of this. What kind of witches would we be if we can't handle a little problem like stolen candy, especially on Halloween?"

The glare of determination glinted in her eyes and the evil smile on her face frightened Daniel, and he stepped off the porch. "Miss Agatha, are you good witches or bad witches?"

Endora picked up her broom, the Curtis Twin Stick, mounted it, and cackled. "Well, now, dearie, that all depends on who's asking. You and your brother wait right here. Agatha and I will sort this out. Ashtoreth, you're with me."

The coal-black cat meowed ran up the broomstick and held onto Endora's dress with her claws. Endora turned to Agatha. "You coming or not?"

"Oh, hell yes. I live for moments like these."

Daniel and Squire watched the brooms vanish into the moonlit sky. Nothing about it seemed strange. It was Halloween, after all, and everyone in town knew that Endora was a witch. Squire sat on the steps, turned his head, and looked at the plastic pumpkin filled with candy that sat on a small table just inside the door. "Danny, you think they'd mind if we ate some of their candy."

"Squire, are you demented? They just flew off on broomsticks. Broomsticks! We aren't doing nothing without asking permission."

"You don't always ask Mom for permission."

"I don't, but Mom can't turn me into a toad. I'd hate to be in Freddy's shoes now."

Agatha and Endora flew higher than they needed to fly, but the night was young, and the moon was bright, and witches so rarely get to enjoy the rush of the wind in their faces on Halloween. They circled around for a while and deliberately tried to position themselves so that any alert resident could photograph them silhouetted against the moon.

"Will the boys be okay on your front porch?' asked Agatha.

"Perfectly fine. I bespelled the front gate. It won't open except to them should they choose to go home. I magicked the candy bowl outside the gate. Any children can only take one piece. If they try for two pieces, their hand won't go into the bowl."

"That's clever."

"It is, isn't it? While the jury might be out on whether I'm a good witch or a bad witch, nobody doubts that I'm a smart witch."

"Or a conceited one."

"Agatha, play nice," said Endora smugly. "You're not conceited if what you say is true. Now, let's find the Kruger boys. We want to be home by midnight. While we don't perform a black mass, lighting a candle to celebrate the end of All Hallows Eve is a tradition I'd hate to miss. Where did you see the boys?"

Agatha spun her Boeing Stratoduster in a quick spin and pointed toward the corner of Elm and Thirteenth Street. "That rust bucket they call a car is parked right there."

Endora straightened her black hat and then gripped her Curtis Twin Stick tightly between her knees. "Hang on, Ashtoreth. We're going in. Divebomb, Agatha."

"I'd love to," Agatha said, and she rolled over to her right and sped straight down. Endora spoke to her cat, "I do hope the brakes on that Boeing broom work."

Ashtoreth mewed an affirmative, and Endora streaked after Agatha.

Agatha pulled upward on her broom, but it didn't respond quickly enough, and she made an inadvertent landing on top of the car, bouncing hard and denting the roof. She shook her fist upward at Endora. "Don't you dare say a word. I'll contact the manufacturer first thing tomorrow."

Inside the car, Freddy spewed chocolate onto the seat, the steering wheel, and the windshield. "What the hell. Was that a bat?"

Mike brushed dozens of bite-sized candy bars onto the floorboard. "Not unless it's a big bat. Big like the fattest Dracula in the world size bat. The roof is dented and look what you've done. You've ruined the upholstery. You better get out and look."

Freddy tried to wipe chocolate off the windshield, but he only made a streaked mess, and he turned on the windshield wipers.

Mike slid his mask to the top of his head. "Moron, the chocolate's on the inside. The wipers won't help. I'll help you clean it."

The brothers scrubbed the glass with empty candy wrappers, the packaging from a couple of kiddie meals, and the dregs from two raspberry slush drinks. They didn't make the glass clearer, but the smear became more uniform.

Endora gently landed on the hood of the car. She peered into the interior, but it was hard to see inside through the gummy mess. She motioned to Agatha, and then, the two of them bounced up and down. Slowly at first, but then faster and harder, tossing the boys and hundreds of candy pieces around inside the car.

Freddy, his face dripping raspberry goo, bounced against the windshield and peeked out of the last remaining un-chocolated spot. "Mike, witch! There's a witch on the hood. Hide."

"Where am I supposed to hide? We're inside a car."

Endora stopped bouncing and tapped on the glass. "Why don't you boys come out and play?"

The boys hunkered down in the front seat.

Endora held out her hand and said, "Fine, have it your way. I understand that you two want some Halloween candy. Okay, here's some candy." She slowly raised her hand and as her hand lifted upward, the level of candy rose inside the car. It reached the boy's knees and then their waists.

Freddy frantically tried to brush away the rising tide of Reese's Pieces, Kisses, Baby Ruths, and Kit-Kat Bars, but the candy kept rising. It reached his chest, and Agatha began bouncing on the roof again. Mike pushed his face as high as he could, but he lifted it too high, and a big bounce smashed his face against the car's roof.

"Damn, Freddy. I tink I brode my nose." He tried to say something else, but the car was almost completely full of Halloween candy, and every time he opened his mouth, a piece of candy filled it. Mike spit out the candy, but he couldn't keep his mouth closed because his nose was bleeding, and the only way he could breathe was through his mouth. He faced a tough decision. Suffocate with his mouth closed or suffocate with a mouth full of Milky Way bars. He put his hands over his mouth and formed a small space free of chocolate and he took a badly needed deep breath. "Freddy, do whad jou want. I'm outta here."

Mike opened the passenger door, and the candy poured out like water running out of a car that had been pulled from a lake, but instead of a drowned body in the cascade, Mike fell out and scrambled across the candy-covered pavement. He slipped and slid on the candy. He staggered, but he didn't fall. The Captain Kirk mask shifted downward over his face. He couldn't see, but once he regained his balance, he ran as fast as he could manage straight into a light pole. He knocked himself out and dropped to the ground.

Agatha did a quick flyby. "He's alive. He's alive." She chanted, "*Dulcia Operuit*," and pieces of Halloween candy flew across the pavement and covered Mike in a thin layer of unopened bite-size treats.

Freddy poured out of the other side of the car in an avalanche of candy. He looked at Endora astride her broomstick and screamed. He ran.

Endora pointed and said, "*Fulmina Dulcia*," meaning lightning bolts of candy. A hailstorm of packaged candies leaped from the ground and pelted Freddy as he ran away.

Freddy saw a police car parked on Mulberry, and he ran toward it, screaming, "Fire, fire, fire!"

Endora stopped the candy assault barely a second before the driver of the police car lit up Freddy with a spotlight. The policeman got out and held up his hand. Freddy stopped and raspberry chocolate goo ran down his pants onto the ground. "Stay right there. You get that mess inside my car, and I'll shoot you. What's going on?"

Freddy didn't answer. He gasped for breath. The other policeman got out of the car and said, "Jim, I heard this candy-coated kid screaming fire. What's your name, son? Where's the fire?"

"I'm Freddy. There ain't no fire."

"Then why were you yelling fire."

"Witches. They attacked us with chocolate. I think they killed my brother over on Elm Street. I yelled fire because if I yelled chocolate, no one would help me."

"Well," said Officer Jim, "Kenny, I think he's got a point there." He ran his flashlight up and down Freddy's body. "Don't you touch my car, either. You look like Willy Wonka threw up on you or that you lost a fight with an Oompa-Loompa. Show us your brother. Elm Street's only two blocks. We'll walk."

Endora filled two large sacks with candy for the Boone boys. "Agatha, we'd best be gone before the police get here. Jim and Kenny were fans of mine when they were boys, but as adults, they tend to see things differently. Do you think that piece of garbage broomstick will fly you back to my house?

"Stop making fun of my Boeing broomstick. It only had one little problem on re-entry," Agatha snapped, and she flew away.

Freddy and the police made a wide circle around the car and the candy-littered street. Jim took one look at Mike and said, "My God, they've killed him, Kenny."

Kenny looked for a clean spot to check Mike's pulse, but he couldn't find one. "No, he's alive. If he wasn't, I'd have said, "He's dead, Jim."

Jim called for an ambulance. "Thank goodness he isn't dead. I really didn't want to write a report using the phrase, death by chocolate."

"I get that. I guess it would make the boys back at the precinct snicker."

"I'm gonna pretend you didn't say that. Should we call a hazmat team?"

'Not for Halloween candy. Like as not, the little ghosts and goblins will clean it up before morning. You wanna book Freddy or let him go?"

"If we book him, we have to touch him. Let him go. I'll call a tow truck for the car. After the ambulance gets here, let's call it a night."

Endora landed near her front porch and looked at the sky, but Agatha was nowhere to be seen. She gave the Boone boys each a large bag of candy. "The Krugers won't bother you again. I expect they've had enough candy to last a lifetime. Run along now. When you grow up and think about being mean to other children, remember how unhappy you were tonight. I'll be watching. I promise."

The boys walked out the gate, and Agatha walked in carrying her Boeing Stratoduster over one shoulder. She threw it on the grass and pointed at Endora. "Not a word. Don't you say one single word!"

"I think the situation speaks for itself."

"I've got to fly home after we light midnight candles. May I borrow your broom?"

Endora thought for a moment, went inside, and rummaged in a closet. She came back with a crooked broomstick. It had twigs instead of straw, and the wood was blackened with age. "Here, you can use this one. It was made by the Montgolfier brothers around 1790. Rumor is that Robespierre used it to escape the guillotine."

Agatha looked at the broom dubiously. "Will it make it to Cincinnati by morning?"

"It should. It pulls to the right and tends to drift in the wind. I never cared for the seat. It's a bit too narrow for a full-bodied woman such as myself."

"Thank you, cousin. I'll see you next Halloween. Your place or mine?"

"Mine, Agatha. We'll ensure that the Kruger boys haven't forgotten their lesson. This is a nice neighborhood, and we don't want another nightmare on Elm Street."

LATE
DELIVERY
ERIKA M SZABO

The clock ticked loudly on the wall of Dimitri's Pizza, signaling the approaching closing time on All Hollow's Eve. Stephanie wearily glanced at it, counting down the minutes until she could finally go home. Meanwhile, Mike vigorously mopped the floors, his movements quick and efficient as he cleaned up the last traces of a busy night. At the counter, Sasha, Mike's younger sister, sat perched on a stool, her attention completely absorbed by the colorful TikTok videos playing on her phone. The soft glow of the screen illuminated her face, casting shadows across her features as she giggled at the latest viral dance challenge. The aroma of the last two freshly baked pizzas lingered in the air, mixing with the faint scent of cleaning products. As Stephanie wiped down tables and refilled condiment bottles, she couldn't help but feel a sense of contentment - this was just another typical evening at Dimitri's, full of familiar sights and smells that brought her comfort and joy.

With a shrill ring, the phone shattered the peaceful sounds of the pizzeria. Stephanie's eyes rolled in exasperation as she begrudgingly reached for the receiver, her fingers already tapping out a familiar greeting.

"Dimitri's Pizza, may I take your order?" Her voice was laced with irritation, but there was only silence on the other end. She repeated herself, growing more annoyed with each passing second. "Hello? Is anyone there?" Still, no response came through the line.

Seeing her frustration, Mike abandoned his station behind the counter and rushed over to her side, his expression reflecting equal parts annoyance and amusement. With a knowing smirk, he tapped a button on the phone and put it on speaker, ready to confront another prank caller.

Then, they were greeted by a very old woman with a deep, gravelly voice on the line. The woman inquired about the type of meat used in their meat lovers' pizza. Stephanie replied, "Pepperoni, sausage, and bacon."

"I want fresh, raw meat," the woman demanded.

"We don't serve raw meat!" Stephanie exclaimed, disgusted.

"Then just bring me a large cheese pizza, and I'll add my own meat," the woman cackled.

Stephanie asked for the woman's last name and address. When Sasha heard the name 'Memy Yagen,',' her face turned pale, and she seemed genuinely frightened.

Despite Sasha's baffling reaction, Stephanie dutifully took down the order, promising swift delivery within the next half-hour. As she made her way to the kitchen to prepare the pizza, she couldn't shake off the unease that had settled in her stomach. Something about the order and Sasha's demeanor had put her on edge. She carefully packed the steaming pizza into a box and headed out to her car, eager to get this strange encounter behind her.

But Sasha followed her out, still engrossed in whatever creepy video she had been watching on her phone. With a shiver, she shared the link with Stephanie, suggesting she watch it while driving. As Stephanie listened to the gory details of the story and realized with growing alarm that she had left the city far behind and was now driving along a desolate country road flanked by tall trees casting eerie shadows in the moonlight. The howling wind and rustling leaves added an ominous soundtrack to Sasha's terrifying tale. Stephanie felt a chill run down her spine as she gripped the steering wheel tighter, her senses on high alert for any signs of danger lurking in the darkness.

As she approached the bridge, the podcast's narrator shared a chilling tale of an old witch who resided in the depths of the woods at the end of a desolate road. *The witch, known as Memy Yagen*, is displayed on the screen as the narrator's voice continued, "The legend says she possesses unimaginable powers. Never, ever say her name!" warned the voice in the video, sending a wave of fear coursing through Stephanie's body. "For if you do, your fate will be sealed."

It's just another silly prank video. There are no witches. She reasoned, but the warning filled her with an unsettling sense of dread.

The winding road was shrouded in darkness, illuminated only by the weak beams of Stephanie's car headlights. She pulled up to the small house nestled among the trees that was shaped like an old leather boot. *What the hell? Who had this crazy idea to build a house like this?* A sense of unease crept over her as she made her way to the door, her footsteps crunching on the gravel path. The door creaked open to reveal an old woman with wrinkled skin and a sinister smile.

Her eyes were dark and piercing, and she wore a tattered woolen cloak that seemed to blend into the shadows. A putrid smell hung in the air around her, causing Stephanie's stomach to turn. Nervously, she stammered out, "Your pizza, Miss... Miss..."

As the old woman's lips curled into a sinister smile, they parted to reveal a row of yellowed, decaying teeth. "Who are you looking for?" she asked in a hoarse, raspy voice.

Stephanie's stomach twisted in knots as she hesitated, her mind flashing back to the warning in the video. She couldn't shake off the feeling of dread that washed over her as she took in the repulsive odor permeating the air around them. It was a mix of decay and something unidentifiable, making her want to gag.

The old woman let out a raspy chuckle, her wrinkled hand extending with a handful of gold coins. The moonlight reflected off her piercing eyes, causing her pupils to dilate and her irises to glow. "So, who is it that you seek?" she asked for the second time, her voice laced with an otherworldly tone.

Stephanie's breath caught in her throat as she tried to resist the compulsion to say the name. But under the mesmerizing gaze of the old woman's eyes, she couldn't help but blurt out, "Memy Yagen." The words hung in the air like ice sickles.

The old woman screeched and lunged at her with gnarled hands, barely missing her wrist. "You're my fresh meat!"

Stephanie broke eye contact with the crazed figure and sprinted back to her car. Her heart pounded in her chest as she fumbled with the key, desperate to start the engine and escape this nightmare. After a few tense moments, the car sputtered to life, and Stephanie floored the gas pedal, leaving behind the deranged woman and her haunting words: *You're my fresh meat!*

As she accelerated away, the ground beneath her shook with a deep rumbling. Glancing at the back-view mirror, Stephanie's heart skipped a beat as she witnessed the cottage rising off its foundation that seemed to have a mind of their own. The boot-shaped cottage was chasing after her, determined to catch her and she saw the old woman standing on the steps of the house. The thunderous sound of giant footsteps echoed in her ears as she sped down the road, adrenaline pumping through her veins.

Just as she reached the bridge, the footsteps suddenly stopped. Stephanie slowed her car cautiously, unsure of what had caused the sudden halt. But before she could fully process the situation, her car was jolted from behind with incredible force. She turned around to see the old woman standing on the back of her car, wielding a bat and ferociously attacking her car. Fear and confusion surged through her as she desperately tried to drive away, but the old woman didn't budge.

With a creaking groan, the old woman lifted her gnarled hands and pounded on the glass window, desperate to get through. But Stephanie had already reached the other side of the bridge, her heart pounding in her chest as she looked back at the old woman who seemed to be suspended in midair, unable to cross an invisible barrier. The moonlight filtering through the trees cast eerie shadows, adding to the tension and fear that filled the air. Stephanie could hear the rustle of leaves and the distant chirping of birds, but all she could focus on was the menacing figure of the old woman retreating. With trembling legs, she continued to drive, her breaths coming out in short gasps as she finally made it to the familiar road, leaving the old woman behind with a shudder of relief and dread.

Stephanie's car screeched to a stop in the parking lot, and she bolted out of the driver's seat, her heart racing with adrenaline. She pushed open the door to the pizza shop with trembling hands and stumbled inside, gasping for air but grateful to be alive. As she recounted the terrifying events to Mike, she pulled out the gold coins from her pocket and placed them on the counter.

Mike's face drained of color as he stared at the coins in disbelief. "There was…that woman called as you were pulling out of the driveway and ordered an additional pizza. She said she had unexpected company."

"What? Where is Sasha?" Stephanie's frantic gaze darted around, searching for her friend.

"She ran outside to tell you, but you were gone already, so she said she'd do the delivery."

"We have to find Sasha!" Stephanie screamed, grabbing Mike's hand, she pulled him toward the door. "That…she's a witch!" Stephanie gasped, recalling the chilling video they had watched the night before. "Every year, a young delivery person disappears and is never found. We must find her!"

Stephanie's mind raced with images of witches and dark magic lurking just beyond their reach. They had to find Sasha before it was too late.

As they neared the spot where the bridge was supposed to span across the river, all they saw was dense forest. No sign of the river and bridge. At the edge of the woods, they found Sasha's abandoned car, its once sleek exterior now mangled and crushed. Panic set in as they frantically searched for Sasha, but she was nowhere to be found. They combed the surrounding woods, every tree and bush becoming a potential hiding place. But they never found her or the elusive house that had lured Stephanie there in the first place. The forest seemed to swallow up any clues or traces of the old witch's existence, leaving nothing behind but unanswered questions and a sense of confusion and panic in the air.

After weeks of unsuccessful searching, they had to give up and accept the undeniable fact that Sasha would never be found. The legend of Memy Yagen became a chilling reality.

HEADLESS
Karen Ovér

"So, will you come with me to visit Miz Flora on Halloween?" Janet grinned at her boyfriend, who rolled his eyes.

"Is that the height of horror in this town? Roll up and see the creepy old lady? I can think of better things to do."

Janet laughed. "If you want to fit in around here, you need to know the local legends. Miz Flora not only knows all of them, she *is* one, herself. Everyone hits Miz Flora's house last on Halloween, to hear her tell the story of the Headless Ghost of Foxfire Creek."

"Does this involve a big black horse and a flaming pumpkin?"

Janet shook her head slowly, her eyes promising mischief. "She'll be our *first* stop, so you can hear the story from someone whose family has passed it down from first-hand accounts."

"How true is it likely to be, then?" Bill laughed, but Janet's expression didn't change.

"Every folk tale has a grain of truth at the core," Janet told him. "That's what Miz Flora says. You'll see."

Bill took her into his arms. "I've got a job waiting for me with a good firm in Houston. We'll get a nice little house off the loop." He patted Janet's belly. "The mother of my son isn't going to live above a hick town ballet studio, teaching a bunch of no talents."

Janet's expression changed, though Bill never saw it. There were many things about Janet that Bill never saw because he was always looking at visions of his own success. He found them preferable to the sight of Janet's hometown and wondered how the hell he'd let her talk him into spending Halloween in the middle of nowhere.

At ten o'clock that night, Janet led him up the steps of a small, neat, frame house surrounded by small, neat flower beds. The gingerbread-trimmed porch was lined with artfully carved Jack-o'-lanterns and a row of costumed children seated at the feet of an old woman.

The creak of her rocking chair played counterpoint to the creak of the oak branches in the night wind. "Y'all wanna hear 'bout the Headless Ghost?" the old woman asked.

"Yes, please, Miz Flora," the children sang in unison.

Bill and Janet sat down on the porch steps. A handful of parents lingered about the lawn, pretending not to listen. Miz Flora leaned forward in her rocker.

"Y'all know why nobody swims in Foxfire Creek?"

"The Headless Ghost!" The children sang.

"That's right," Miz Flora cackled. "That ol' ghost don't want no one messin' round the Foxfire, not down by the old trestle, 'cause that's where he lost his head. Went sneakin' through the pines to see his gal, took the shortcut 'cross the trestle, got himself caught by the midnight express. Not no diesel train, no. Big steam engine, whistle screamin' like a banshee as it come up on the trestle, big ol' headlight, like the full moon fallin' out of the sky, right on top of him. Pistons pumpin', drivin' rods pushing those big steel wheels so fast they're a blur. Some said it was the drivin' rods tore him up, stroke by stroke, till there was nothin' left but his head, wedged between the spokes of a drivin' wheel. Crew found it there at the next water stop, but no one ever found the body. Some say his head got tore off clean, and the body fell right back into Foxfire Creek. Say it happened so fast, he didn't even know he'd lost his head. Which is why if you look down into the water on a full moon night, you can see what's left of that ol' trestle, and you can see *him*, still swimmin' round down there, lookin' for his head. You go swimmin' there, that Headless Ghost, he'll grab *your* head!"

The children scrambled back, shrieking with delighted fear, as the old woman rocked forward with clawed fingers reaching for their heads.

Miz Flora stood up, and the children gathered up their bags, lining up for their treats. Within minutes, the street was empty as the little goblins faded into the night. Porch lights went out, and Bill suppressed a shudder as darkness and silence closed in around them.

"You kids want a nightcap before you go for your walk?" Flora ushered them through her front door, and on into her kitchen. "Wanna try a nip of the family 'shine, Bill?"

"Now, Miz Flora," Janet half warned, half teased. "You know I'm gonna take him down along Foxfire Creek. That 'shine of yours sneaks up on a fella. He'll set off feelin' fine and be stumblin' drunk just in time for something dreadful to happen, just like that Headless Ghost."

"Dandelion wine, then," Miz Flora replied, guiding them into her kitchen. She poured three small glasses of golden liquid and joined them at the table.

Bill took a sip of the dandelion wine. It went down surprisingly smooth. He found himself staring at the Halloween centerpiece, a skull with flowers protruding from the eye sockets and a black rose between its grinning teeth. He gulped down the rest of his wine. "So, this Headless Ghost, who was he? Or is he just a story?"

"He was my granddaddy," Miz Flora said with a grin. "Walter Meeks was his name. No 'count drunk, he was. Come sneakin' over that trestle and up to our old home place. Got my grandmama in trouble, then got himself killed before her daddy could even load the shotgun. Janet will show you where it happened, right down there at the bottom of the old garden. Some round here say Walter got lucky, not havin' to marry my grandmama. Some say he wouldn't have lived through the weddin' night, anyhow, since Grandmama already had what she wanted from him. A girl child to carry on the family legacy. Just like Janet will have a girl child to carry on her legacy at the ballet school. Another glass, Bill?"

"Don't mind if I do, Miz Flora, but then we need to get going. Janet's got plans for me tonight." Bill let out a suggestive chuckle, then knocked back a second glass of wine.

Janet lit an old-fashioned railroad lantern, which threw murky light through alternating red and green lenses. "Time for your ghost tour of Foxfire Creek." She smiled, her eyes promising, her forefinger beckoning.

Flora showed them out the back door. "Mind where you go," she warned. "Those banks are mighty treacherous."

Bill laughed. "Yeah, and the Headless Ghost might get me." He followed along in the shadows thrown by the lantern through the rows of a huge, strange garden. He reached for a tall stalk bearing many blooms, letting his fingers brush the flowers.

They reached the bottom of the garden and went up through a stand of pines. Janet held the lantern high. "This is the old poison garden. Miz Flora comes from a long line of conjure women. Don't touch anything. There's the old house she grew up in. And over there, that's where the first still was. Foxfire Moonshine. It's made in town, now."

"What are we doing here, Janet?"

"You need to understand who I am, Bill. Under these pines, this is where Meeks lost his head. This is where Miz Flora's grandmama let him catch her. If you listen, you can hear the Foxfire running. Sometimes, you can hear that old train whistle, too. Come on, I'll show you where the train hit him. Be careful."

***

Miz Flora sat on her front porch, listening to the wind whistling in the pines. A descant over the creaking oak sheltering her house. What might have been the shriek of an old steam whistle morphed into the siren of an emergency vehicle.

A few hours later, the sheriff walked Janet up to Flora's front porch. "Helluva shock, Miz Flora. That city boy of hers fell into the Foxfire right on top of that busted-up trestle. Broke his neck so bad it nearly tore his head off."

Flora took the pale girl into her arms. "You stay here tonight, honey. We'll sort everything out in the morning. Good night, Lamar."

"Good night, Miz Flora." The sheriff touched his hat, retreating into the darkness.

Flora tucked Janet up with a cup of cocoa. "Don't you worry. You and I and the boys at the ballet school, we'll raise up that child of yours just fine."

"I know, Miz Flora. I kept telling Bill he needed to understand me. All he did was laugh. Just like he laughed at the Headless Ghost."

Miz Flora plumped Janet's pillows. "He shouldn't have underestimated you, my dear, or where you come from."

Downstairs in the kitchen, Flora lifted two shots of Foxfire Moonshine in salute to the skull on her table. Knocking one back, she poured the other over the skull. It burst into bright blue flames, devouring the alcohol. "Happy Halloween, Granddaddy. Say hey to Bill."

182

FALL
MARKET
VICTORIA
ADAMS

Elenore parked her car and gathered her basket and hat. The breeze coming off the ocean was cool, with just enough lift for a few colorful kites. The sun sparkled on the gentle surf making her smile as she took a deep breath and set off with determination to take her time and enjoy this fall day. It had been a month since she had moved to this small coastal town. Was this a place she could stay, or was it time to pack up again?

She strolled through the farmer's market with her basket dangling from her arm. For such a small community, there was quite a variety of fruits and veggies. A few booths sported homemade baking products, and a few others were selling the things needed to "put things up" for future consumption. The local artisans displayed an array of goods in multiple mediums.

With cautious optimism, she decided to look for some piece of art that might cheer up her small cabin and maybe provide inspiration. A vase in the stall of a potter caught her eye. The vase was a beautiful hand-thrown piece with an hourglass shape, open enough at the neck for a nice-sized bouquet. Encircling the wide base was a collection of stylized cages with birds flying free or preening in the open cage doors. The whimsical style made her feel light. She smiled as she picked up the piece to check the price. Not bad for a hand-crafted work of art.

She was startled by a voice behind her. "The vase seems to make you happy. May I wrap it for you so you can get it home safely?"

Elenore turned to see an elderly, slightly bent woman smiling up at her. "Yes, I do love the vase. It makes me feel…optimistic."

The old woman nodded. "Then you must also have the companion wall hanging. Calligraphy on ivory parchment. I mix my own ink and press the parchment myself. Here, would you like to read it?"

Elenore set the vase back on the shelf and reached for the rolled-up paper. Unfurling it she read the words of "Caged Bird" by someone named Maya Angelou. "A free bird leaps on the back of the wind…" Finishing the poem, she realized she was nearly breathless, the last line making her heart race. "…for the caged bird sings of freedom." The words echoed in her mind. Free. What did free look like feel like? Was it a prize she would ever claim?

The shopkeeper spoke in that low voice that only your best friend uses when they are there to support you but maybe not provide a million solutions, none of which seem possible. "So, do you like it? You may have it to go with the vase. Both, for the price of the vase."

Elenore looked up from the vase and caught the old woman's gaze. Unable to speak, she simply nodded.

Several minutes later, she was back in the bustling crowds, feeling disoriented and exposed. Her heart still raced in her chest, and her vision blurred with the sudden glare. To calm her nerves, she visited the veggie stalls to collect interesting candidates for the coming week's meals. She spent considerable time choosing selections at the spice and herb stall. When her heart and hands had steadied, she began to wander through the fair, not sure of what she was looking for. Her back straightened as she searched the stalls nearby. Flowers would be nice, a bouquet for the new vase.

Her curiosity led her to a new vendor. At least she couldn't remember seeing this one before. But then, she couldn't recall the old woman from previous trips, either. Elenore looked back at the way she had come and shook her head when she couldn't locate the stall. Well, it was crowded, and maybe the old woman only worked half a day. She turned and continued toward the flower merchant.

The aroma of several fresh blooms reached her before she reached the booth. Stepping out of the glare of the early afternoon sun, she adjusted her floppy hat to better see the offerings in the shady booth. There was a cool breeze blowing, and her well-developed radar began to ping. There was something unsettling about the small and crowded space. *Oh, for goodness sake, I'm just unnerved by that old woman looking at me with her knowing smile. I'll be fine. I just want to find some flowers for the vase.*

Browsing through the offerings with intent, she jumped when a male voice behind her asked if he could help.

"I—I'm not sure. I just purchased a vase in another booth, and I'd like to find something to build an arrangement. Are these flowers freshly picked? I'd like something native to the area that might last a few days."

The man smiled as his eyes grew more intense. "I live some distance away, but I pick my stock early in the morning and keep it cool during the drive. You might feel the fan I set up to keep the flowers cool under the shade. These are all plants that are native to our area. Are you looking to create a specific mood or stay with a particular color pallet?"

He seemed sincere, but his look didn't put her at ease. At least she knew why there was a chilly breeze. He was still watching her.

Elenore laughed nervously. "Fall colors, I think I'd like fall colors and long stems. Maybe some greenery for fill."

He was still for a moment, then nodded. "Yes, I know just the perfect thing." Leading her to a far corner, he began to gather blooms. "Do you know how wide your vase is?"

Silently, she pulled the bundled package from her basket. As she held it out to him, he ran a hand over the wrapping and nodded.

"Looks to be from Miss Romona's stall. Excellent choice. I think these will do quite nicely. Were you aware that many believe that flowers have attributes? Something they represent other than life and beauty."

Eleanor shook her head. "No, I wasn't. What have you picked for me?" She believed, somewhere inside, that he had indeed picked these blossoms just for her.

He smiled as he wrapped the selections in brown paper. "These should be fine until you get home, that is, if you are nearby. Just keep them out of the sun." Then he pointed to each of the three plants he had chosen and explained. "The black-eyed Susans represent justice. I felt from your hesitancy, you could use some. The witch-hazel represents healing and protection because after justice, perhaps you could use both. The brilliantina should provide you with nice fill and a bit more color. I think the oranges and greens on the leaves will go nicely with the blooms."

She stood for a moment, almost afraid to put the package in her basket. Reaching for her wallet, she provided payment, retrieved the lovely blooms, and thoughtfully walked away.

Feeling deeply uneasy, she decided her shopping tour should end. She was protecting the fresh flowers, right? She wasn't leaving because she felt seen just now. Seen in ways she had not experienced since she'd left her partner several months ago. Her shoulders

186

tightened as she considered her anxiety. Would she have to move yet again?

In an effort to calm her nerves, she forced herself to focus on the mundane. She had some favorite tea, and one baker was offering warm coffee cake. Keeping her pace to a stroll, she finally reached the entrance. She looked for the potter's stall but couldn't find it. *I must be turned around, I thought this was the lane I took at first, but I just don't see it. Oh, well. I like what I have, and I need to get home.*

She stowed her basket in the back seat of her car where the sun could not reach it and its cargo. Before she settled into the driver's seat, she turned back toward the fair. She knew the layout. These days, she went nowhere without scoping out the situation and identifying escape routes. She could see neither of the booths she had visited and if memory served, they should have been in sight. Well, with her jangled nerves, maybe she misjudged. But no, there were empty spaces where the flower booth and the potter should be. Well, then. Maybe her unrest had warned them, and they had left. Her skin tingled, and she sincerely hoped she would see neither merchant again. She was not up for more mystery.

Reaching her current hide-away, she set her basket on the kitchen counter, put the food away, and then unwrapped the vase. The artwork was beautiful, and she again felt the lightness of spirit as she pulled the flowers from their wrapper. She took her time arranging the selections and smiled at her creation. She filled the vase with water and set it on her small kitchen table. Her fingers traced the patterns of birds freed from their cages. Her phone rang.

Glancing at the screen, she saw that the number was blocked. Shuddering, she knew that no one she would want to talk to would block their number. They would know better. With a shaking hand, she put the phone down and took a deep breath. *Okay, I'll take a shower and give it an hour. Maybe I'll pack just in case there's another call. He couldn't find me, could he? Shower, get in the shower.*

Elenore kept her shower short—too nervous to be in a vulnerable state. Fully dressed, she went back to the kitchen and picked up her phone. There was a missed call, but this number she knew. The only person in the world that even knew which direction she had taken when she left. Hands shaking again, she punched in the number.

"Ann? You called. Is there something wrong?" She held her breath while she waited for the answer. She could be packed and ready to leave in less than 15 minutes. She had way too much practice at it.

Her friend's voice came through the speaker. "Elenore, there's been an accident. I don't have a lot of details. I just know that he was texting and sped through a red light. He was t-boned by a semi. His sister called me, screaming that it was all your fault. Evidently, someone thought they had seen you, and he was trying to get there." Her friend was quiet for several beats. "Elenore, I called to tell you that you are free. He is gone. He can't hurt you anymore. You can come home."

Elenore stood in her tiny kitchen and her eyes fell on the new vase with its flying and preening birds. With her free hand, she unfurled the little scroll and read the poem again. Whispering, she recited the last few lines, "for the caged bird sings of freedom." She was free, truly free.

"No, Ann, I think I'll stay here and build something new. I feel— protected here."

The Authors

Erika M Szabo

https://authorerikamszabo.com

Erika loves to dance to her own tunes and follow her dreams, introducing her story-writing skills and her books that are based on creative imagination with themes such as magical realism, alternate history, urban fantasy, cozy mystery, sweet romance, and supernatural stories. Her children's stories are informative and educational and deliver moral values in a non-preachy way.

Lorraine Carey

https://authorlorrainecarey.blogspot.com/

Lorraine Carey is a reading specialist and an Award-Winning Author. She was living in California until fate whisked her off to Grand Cayman. She currently lives in Florida. Her love for paranormal stories began at a young age, and is no stranger to the paranormal, having encountered unexplainable events that are woven into her stories.

Martha Perez

https://marthaperez.info/

Martha Perez was born in raised in Los Angeles, CA. She now lives in West Covina, CA, with her husband, Sal Andalon, and their dogs, Toby and Bella. She has a son, a daughter, and two granddaughters. Her hobbies include reading, writing, exercising, and taking long walks.

David W. Thompson

https://www.david-w-thompson.com

David is a multiple award-winning author, Army veteran, and graduate of UMUC. He's a multi-genre writer and a member of the Horror Writers' Association, and the Science Fiction & Fantasy Writers Association. When not writing, Dave enjoys family, kayaking, fishing, hiking, hunting, winemaking, and woodcarving.

Shebat Legion

Her work can be found wherever fine books are sold.

Shebat Legion is an award-winning, internationally best-selling, consummate storyteller/producer/publisher whose quirky tales have appeared in numerous anthologies of various genres, and offerings of her work have been archived on the moon via The Lunar Codex associated with NASA.

Robert Allen Lupton

https://robertallenlupton.blogspot.com

Robert Allen Lupton is retired and lives in New Mexico. He has three novels, seven short story collections, and three edited anthologies available in print and audio versions. Over 2000 of his Edgar Rice Burroughs themed drabbles and articles are located on erbzine.com

R. A. "Doc" Correa

www.goldenboxbooks.com/ra-doc-correa.html

A retired US Army military master parachutist, retired surgical technologist, and retired computer scientist. He's an award-winning poet and author. "Doc" has had poems published in multiple books and had stories published in Bookish Magazine and Your Secret Library. His first novel, Rapier, won a Book Excellence award and was given a Reader's Favorite five-star review.

E.V. Emmons

https://eclark46.wixsite.com/-evemmons

E.V. Emmons lives in Ontario. Author of the novels ETERNITY AWAITS, THE SINISTRATI, and the writer's guide, 'WRITE HERE, WRITE NOW!' As a contributor to several anthologies, her work even made it to the Moon with the Lunar Codex Program aboard lander Odysseus in February 2024. Available on Amazon.

Karen Ovér

https://balletsandbogeys.weebly.com/golemwerks.html

Karen Ovér is back in Texas after more than a decade in New York City. Her latest works appear in the anthologies The Book of Carnacki, The Legion Press, Dark Yonder #6, and the forthcoming Arkham Institutions, available late 2024 from Dragon's Roost Press.

James Harper

His work can be found wherever fine books are sold.

A transplanted native in a city full of them, James Harper is a bestselling horror writer living with his daughter in a suburb just north of Washington DC. His love of music is only rivaled by his passion for film, but both take a backseat when a Phillies game's on.

Victoria Adams

https://victoriasreadingalcove.com

Adams lives and works in the resplendent Pacific Northwest. She spends her time with her characters and a feline named Sir Linus. She has published two nonfiction titles and contributed to anthologies of fiction and poetry. Her exploration of the world and ideas, in general, can be found at victoriasreadingalcove.com.

The Holiday Edition is coming in December

Most liked stories in What If #1, #2, and #3

What If #1

Lost in the Woods by Erika M Szabo

A young police officer enters the woods to find a missing woman, but it takes all her mental strength to deal with what she finds.

She Waits by Lorraine Carey

During a class field trip to a historical site in the Caribbean, a curious student encounters a lonely ghost who does not want her to leave.

What If? #2

The Zanna by David W. Thompson

A potential stepmother and stepdaughter seek common ground at the family's rustic retreat. Will the past return to haunt them? Only Zanna knows...

Don't Whistle Back by Erika M Szabo

Milena visits her grandfather in Mexico and wonders why he has a rope with seven knots tied to the door. She finds out soon enough!

What If? #3

Unsung Heroes y Erika M Szabo

If people knew what the biker gang did and were not expecting any reward or recognition, these unsung heroes would be celebrated by many.

I Love You Forever by Martha Perez

Can their love endure? Nicole, battling cancer, finds hope with Noah. Will they overcome life's challenges and keep their vow to love forever?

CAREFUL WHAT
YOU WISH FOR
DAVID W. THOMPSON

Robert Allen Lupton
BROOMSTICKS &
CHOCOLATE

ERIKA M SZABO
BURDENS of
IMMORTALITY

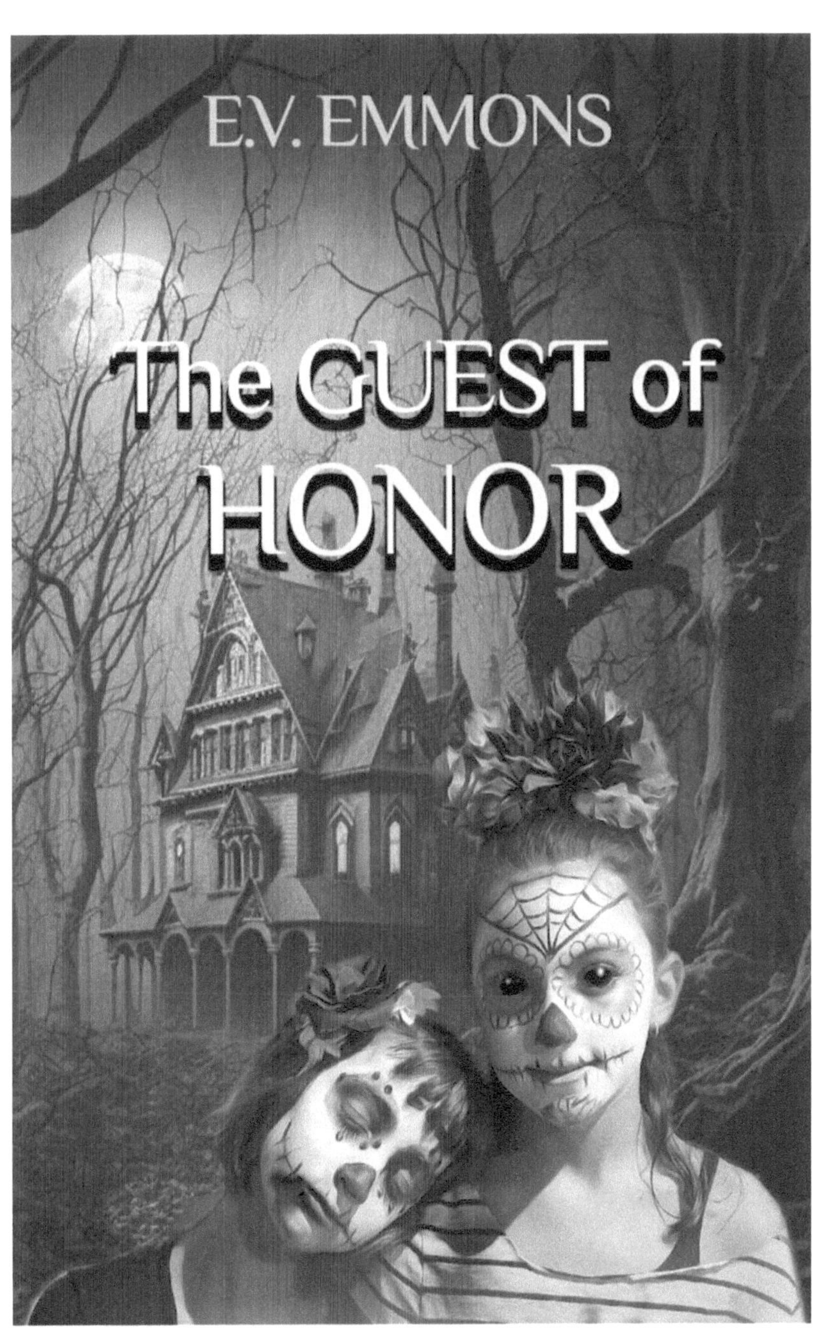

E.V. EMMONS
The GUEST of HONOR

HEADLESS
Karen Ovér

Lorraine Carey
The Doll That
Had it All

Table of Contents